Dead Men Can Kill

Special Limited Edition

116 of 200 copies

FIRST EDITION

Shawn,
Hope you enjoy the book!
Bob Doerr

Also by Bob Doerr

Cold Winter's Kill

is a fast paced thriller that takes place in the scenic mountains of Lincoln County, New Mexico and throws Jim West into a race against time to stop a psychopath who abducts and kills a young blonde every Christmas...

ISBN: 978-1-59095-762-2

A Jim West™ Mystery / Thriller

Dead Men

Can Kill

Bob Doerr

TotalRecall Publications, Inc.

United States   Canada   United Kingdom

Exclusive worldwide content publication / distribution by TotalRecall Publications.
1103 Middlecreek Friendswood, Texas 77546   281-992-3131   281-482-5390 Fax
6 Precedent Drive Rooksley, Milton Keynes MK13 8PR, UK
1385 Woodroffe Av Ottawa, ON K2G 1V8

ISBN: 978-1-59095-758-5

Printed in the United States of America with simultaneously printings in Canada, and the United Kingdom.

1 2 3 4 5 6 7 8 9 10

FIRST EDITION

With love to my number one support staff:
Leigh, Emily, Angee, and Kallie.

PROLOGUE

Seeing blood doesn't bother me, I had seen it many times before, but something about being alone in the middle of nowhere with the top half of my body inside the empty interior of a bloody Suburban gave me the creeps. I instinctively pulled my head out and slammed the door. I knew it was a mistake as soon as I did it. First rule of evidence, don't disturb the crime scene. A little thing, but I felt like a rookie. I shouldn't have closed the door. I was beginning to think I wasn't in charge.

I took a few breaths and looked out over the front hood of the vehicle, down the ravine and up the other side. No indication of movement anywhere. The SUV looked okay from what I could see. I turned away from the vehicle, maybe to head back, maybe to look around. I did neither immediately. I gasped. There just fifteen feet from where I was standing sat Rick Jimenez, the other reporter, as he had described himself that morning, for the town's newspaper. His face was contorted and covered with dried blood. His white shirt completely soaked in blood now drying in the hot sun. He was dead.

It has been ten years since the death of Rick Jimenez and the others but I have only now evolved to the point that I can tell the story. I know I am not culpable for the actions of others, but I also know that I unintentionally started the process that led to that tragic sequence of events. It's been a guilt that has slowly gnawed on me over this past decade.

I can still remember how it began with my peaceful drive to the university in Albuquerque during the summer of 1999. It was shortly after my retirement from the Air Force, my divorce and my move back to New Mexico. The university was in its summer session and the sprawling campus was fairly quiet when I arrived. Dr. Francisco Anaya's criminology course was attended by as many working adults as it was by full time students. It was the second time Dr. Anaya had asked me to be a guest lecturer.

My pension from the Air Force was enough to cover my routine expenses. However, I felt like I had to do something with myself and it was always easy to find a use for the extra money I picked up by making an occasional presentation at various colleges, or even a civic organization or two, in the region. My lectures normally focused on the use of forensic hypnosis in criminal investigations. I was proud of myself for selecting the topic because it seemed to be a hit with all the classes that heard it. Dr. Anaya was not the only professor who had invited me back.

I also got a kick out of the fact that I, personally, had never hypnotized anyone during my twenty years in criminal investigations and counterintelligence. Yet here I was now, teaching a group of aspiring criminologists all about it. I had observed its use in enough investigations to appreciate its utility and to understand its methodology. After leaving the Air Force, I even took a course on the subject in Washington DC. As far as I was concerned, I was more than qualified to spend two hours in front of a classroom and talk about forensic hypnosis.

My mistake was getting involved in practical demonstrations.

Chapter 1

I normally had no trouble finding a volunteer to be hypnotized in front of a group of peers and I was always amazed how frequently the volunteer was female. I tried to imagine what that statistic meant but never could figure out a logical answer. Perhaps because this was a summer class with a mix of college students and working professionals there to further their education, no one volunteered. I therefore reinforced what all school students - and church goers – know: don't sit in the front row or you may get called on. I asked the only person in the front row if he would mind being a guinea pig for the audience. With a reluctant grin, he said okay.

"Luke Fenster, from Denton," he responded to my request that he identify himself to the class. Denton was a small New Mexico town, situated on the old Route 66, and now I-40, about sixty miles west of the Texas state line. "I'm a junior and I hope to get a job with the FBI when I graduate."

"Please take a seat and relax." I requested and then turned back to the class.

The room was cool, in stark contrast to the heat outside. I had the lights turned down just enough to encourage Luke Fenster to relax, though I hoped not low enough to encourage the audience to sleep. Actually, this was the one part of my presentation that usually kept everyone awake.

"As I mentioned before in my presentation, unlike what you may have seen in the movies, or heard about from your friends, the hypnotist can rarely cause post-hypnotic suggestions or make people quack like a duck. It really can't make people do what they would not do in the first place. Its potential in law enforcement is its ability to draw out information from a witness or a victim that may have been forgotten, misplaced in the mind, or blocked out because of shock or emotional trauma.

The best example I can remember from my days as an investigator was a witness' ability to recall a license plate number that solved an attempted murder. The witness had seen the tag but kept getting confused and frustrated when he tried to recall the numbers. Through hypnotism, he was able to relax and methodically work through the sequence of numbers."

I had heard of other more exciting examples, but the one with the license plate numbers was one I personally witnessed. Plus, it was a very simple example that didn't over glamorize hypnosis. I knew there were legal drawbacks to using forensic hypnotism, and while I didn't delve too much into them I tried to at least make each class aware of the pitfalls.

"What I intend to do with Luke, here, is simply take him back through a series of birthdays that he has experienced and see how far back his memories can remain graphic." I positioned myself along side of Luke so the students could see what I was doing, as well as seeing Luke. He reclined in the chair and shut his eyes.

"You need to have your eyes open, Luke. Just relax and watch my old watch, just like in the movies." Using an old watch was not necessary; in fact the pros don't use anything at all. I just found this prop seemed to work well and was normally appreciated by my audience. "Keep watching the watch and let your arms and legs relax. Do you know anything about yoga, Luke?"

He shook his head no.

"Well, we want to follow a similar method here, so just let your whole body relax. Just like going to sleep but keep your eyes open and watch the watch. Listen to my voice, Luke. Focus only on my watch and my voice. That's good, Luke, you're doing fine, let everything go limp. It's okay to get sleepy. Just try to focus on the watch and my voice." I worked hard to keep my voice in a monotone and, fortunately, the rest of the students in the room remained quiet.

I repeated my instructions to Luke for about two minutes before I felt comfortable that he was in a trance. "Tell us your full name, Luke." Although I was never positive, I thought I could tell if my subjects were hypnotized by just asking a few questions and observing how they responded.

"Luke Anthony Fenster," he replied. His voice did sound a bit different and someone from the class "ooooed." I turned and gave a nasty look in the direction of the sound. Too much noise from the audience could easily break a trance.

"How long have you lived in Denton?" I asked softly.

"All my life."

"Who do you live with there?"

"Just my grandmother," he answered.

I stifled an urge to ask him what happened to his parents and went on to the "meat" of the demonstration. "Describe your sixteenth birthday party, Luke."

A small smile again crossed Luke's face. "My granny threw a pool party for me and my friends at the municipal pool. It was fun. There must have been ten kids there. It was hot; the weatherman on the radio said it was over a hundred degrees that day." I couldn't resist turning to the class and raising my index finger to accentuate Luke's specific recall of something that he heard on the radio that day.

"Okay, Luke, just relax some more. Take a deep breath. Everything is so comfortable." I waited about ten seconds. "Now, let's go back to your tenth birthday party, Luke. Did any friends come over to celebrate it with you?" Usually I could go back to the eight to ten year old range without any problems, but preferred to hit on ten as my second stop because it invariably was a year I received good recall from my subjects.

"Danny, Steven, Lester, and Mark were at my party. Granny took us all to the Pizza Palace." Luke answered without any hesitation.

I decided to take a gamble here. "Do you remember what you wore that day, Luke?"

"Yes," he responded, again without any hesitation, "we all wore cowboy gear because we had just come from the junior rodeo."

I turned to the class, again making a mark in the air with my finger. "I know you are sleepy, Luke. You are so comfortable. Let me just ask you one more question. Concentrate, Luke. Concentrate only on my voice. Can you remember anything from your second birthday?"

Luke was silent for a second. I really did not expect him to recall anything from so far back and for a moment I thought he may have actually fallen asleep. "There was a pretty cake, my mom was there, and she had made such a pretty cake. And, AAGH!! No! NO!" Luke screamed in such a shrill voice that I nearly jumped out of my chair.

"Luke, snap out of it. Snap out of it... it's okay, it's me, you can wake up now," I was actually shaking Luke and not realizing it until Dr. Anaya grabbed my arm and asked if everything was all right. Luke looked up at me and out at the class. Although he looked pale, he responded that he was fine.

"Luke, go get yourself a drink of water," Dr. Anaya instructed. Luke lumbered out of the classroom. The rest of the students were talking loudly to each other and asking questions of me and Dr. Anaya about what happened. I began telling them I wasn't sure, but Dr. Anaya interrupted me and told all the students that they had had enough fun for one day and that class was over.

Dr. Anaya walked me out to my car. "Don't worry about the excitement," he said, "I'll probably have more students than you can shake a stick at next term thanks to your little demonstration in there. You obviously made him remember something that scared the *miedo*, excuse my Latin, out of him. If he was really remembering back when he was two, though, that could have been almost anything. My two year old grand daughter has a fit every time a fly comes next to her."

I acknowledged that Dr. Anaya was probably correct. However, I would have felt better if I could have at least seen Luke before I drove off. He had not come back to the classroom and was nowhere to be seen when we had left the room.

My drive home was not as tranquil as my drive to the

university had been that morning.   This was my first
demonstration that ended on such a strange note. I couldn't
help but think of Luke and to hope that he was alright. His
reaction was on my mind for the next four hours as I tried to
imagine what may have caused it.

Chapter 2

The next few days were uneventful for me. I worked on the yard and the wood work on the outside of my house. Luke was still on my mind. To satisfy my lingering curiosity, I called Dr Anaya the following Monday.

"I'm glad you called, Jim. I'm getting a little concerned myself. Luke never returned to class on Friday. A friend of his told me that Luke left the campus on Friday and that he had not been seen since."

"Where did he say his home was, Doc?" I asked. I knew he had mentioned it during the demonstration, but at the time it wasn't really relevant to me.

"Denton, shouldn't be too far from you," he responded. "Are you thinking about going up there? We could have someone call him from here, it would be simple enough."

"No, don't do that. I feel kind of responsible and it looks like a slow week ahead for me. I'll just take a drive up there tomorrow. It's a small town. You wouldn't know the address would you?"

"Hold on a minute," replied Dr. Anaya, "yes, here it is: 335 Lima Street, Denton, New Mexico. Let me know what you find."

I told him I would and hung up the phone. Something nagged at the back of my mind telling me not to wait until the next day to follow up on Luke. In the past I paid attention to these little warnings, but I wasn't operational now. That was all behind me and my semi-retirement was supposed to be relaxing and healthy.   Not the time to get excited about hunches, deadlines, and danger. The odd job once in a while to stay busy and maybe a little fishing and golf; keep the blood pressure down and these days one could live to be a hundred. It all sounded good. But, I couldn't keep Luke out of my mind. Why did I feel that something wasn't right?

All that night, I tossed and turned. I woke up early, fed Chubs my "Heinz 57" dog, and headed off to Denton.

Denton was a sleepy little town that existed only because travelers every now and then needed gas, food and lodging. It was one of the few real blips on the old Route 66, now Interstate 40, between Amarillo and the suburbs of Albuquerque. There was also a small state road that ran north – south through Denton. It was a narrow two lane road, seemingly going nowhere. It was the road on which I approached Denton.

I actually enjoyed these old state roads. Many of them stretched for hundreds of miles through the state. Frequently you could drive on them for miles without seeing another car or person. Early on most mornings, however, if you timed it just right, these roads could be a busy with tractors and trucks all returning to the ranches and fields for the day's work ahead.

I approached Denton from the south at approximately eight in the morning. It was going to be a beautiful day. Only a few small clouds interrupted what was otherwise a perfectly blue sky. As I came down off the caprock into the valley where Denton sat, two prairie antelope bolted from the highway to the protection of the sagebrush.

The rocks of the caprock glistened in the morning sun, casting long shadows across the mesa's slope. A perfect place to film a "cowboy" movie I thought and wondered if any films were ever made out here. If not, the folks out in Hollywood were really missing out. It was easy for me to imagine a wagon train moving along in the valley and then someone looking up and seeing the Indians on horseback on the ridge line watching them.

Actually it was only during rare periods of the past that travelers through the west faced real danger. Those were the periods of time when marauding bands of renegade Apaches or Comanches would terrorize the territory. Driving through this scenic land, I didn't have the slightest realization that a different, but just as deadly danger, now stalked the unwary traveler through this part of New Mexico.

By the time I reached Denton the town was already awake and active. The large truck stops were doing a brisk business and the Pancake House and its clones were sucking in the breakfast crowd. I decided to join them. I wasn't sure where Lima Street was but I figured someone working in the Pancake House could easily point out the directions I needed.

I ordered coffee and a small stack of buttermilk pancakes. I wasn't particularly hungry but thought I might as well get something to eat in exchange for the information I would want. The restaurant was typical of those catering to the tourist crowd that might pass through any region of New Mexico. There were little baskets of western trinkets for sale by the cash register, paintings of the old Wild West on the walls, and most of the meals were named after characters made more popular by television than anything else. Booths aligned the walls and small tables with vinyl cushioned chairs filled the interior spaces of the restaurant. My waitress was an attractive lady in a sky blue uniform, with brown hair and a name tag that said Sue. She was more than happy to explain to me that Lima Street was a small road that ran west off of North Sixth Street. If I was to head to Albuquerque, Sixth Street was the last paved road turning off of the interstate before I left city limits.

The pancakes weren't bad and the coffee was good. Combine that with Sue's pleasant personality and willingness to give me directions, I left a generous tip and headed towards the cash register to pay my bill. As the cashier was ringing up my bill, I noticed two uniformed policemen walk into the restaurant. Immediately a number of the employees and some of the customers stopped what they were doing and surrounded the officers.

"What's going on?" I asked the cashier.

"Not sure, sir, but I heard there was a murder in town last night. I imagine they may be asking the police if they caught the killer yet. This is usually a quiet town. My guess is that is what all the excitement is about."

I waited for the change from my ten dollar bill and then walked past the crowd by the front door and out to my car. From the bits and pieces I heard as I walked by the police officers, I figured the cashier's guess was correct. Remarks such as "a real tragedy", "a shame", and "hope you catch who did it" were comments I had heard myself many times in the past, usually when I was briefing people about a serious crime.

Murder, if that was what it was, is common in big cities, but out here in the small towns of the southwest it is pretty rare. Usually when murders did occur, they were crimes of passion and the police had a pretty good resolution rate in bringing justice its due.

As I pulled out of the restaurant's parking lot, though, I didn't care for the fact that the nagging at the back of my mind was beginning to spread down my spine. I reached back and rubbed the back of my neck but it did little good.

I had no trouble finding Lima Street and was busy trying to read the numbers on the houses when I noticed the police cars and the crime scene tape sealing off a house about a hundred yards down the road.

I wanted to turn around right then and go home. I didn't want to find out what my imagination was already telling me, but I drove on. I knew it was Luke's house before I saw the numbers on the old metal mailbox that leaned precariously out over the curb. I stopped the car and stared at the house. I saw movement inside through the windows but no one was outside in the yard.

"Can I help you?" The question shot in through my open window. I almost jumped through the moon roof. I think my seat belt was the only thing that kept me in the seat. I tried to regain my composure and smiled at the deputy sheriff who had apparently approached me from the house across the road.

"You startled me," I felt silly but I didn't want him to read too much into my reaction, "Can you tell me what happened?"

"What are you doing here?" he responded. "You're not from around here, are you? Why don't you step out of the car for a minute so we can talk."

I didn't like the deputy's overreaction but I knew better than to irritate him. I got out of the car as he called and talked to someone briefly on his radio. I started to identify myself when he cut me off. "Wait for Sheriff Gibbs," and he pointed at a tall slender man in a crisp, clean uniform walking out the front door of Luke's house.

"What's up?" the Sheriff asked, as much to me as to the deputy.

"I'm Jim West, Sheriff. I drove up here this morning from Clovis to see Luke Fenster."

"What's your business with Luke?"

"He attended a lecture I gave in Albuquerque a few days ago. It's a long story, but after my presentation, Luke left the college and did not return. I wanted to speak to him to see if something I had said or done had been the cause of his leaving the school."

"You haven't seen him since the day of your class in Albuquerque?"

"No, and why these questions Sheriff, has something happened?" I asked, already knowing it was a dumb question and not really liking the way three more deputies had come out and were staring at me.

"Luke and his grandmother were killed last night. They apparently interrupted a burglary, at least that's our best guess at the moment. We don't have much to work on, mister, what did you say your name was?"

"Jim West," I replied. I tried to stay calm but the hairs on the back of my neck were flashing me all types of signs I didn't like.

"Well, Mr. West, I would like to talk to you some more

about this lecture of yours, but not here and not now. Think you could come down to the station around two this afternoon?" asked the Sheriff.

"Sure," I replied. One of the deputies was behind my car copying down the license tag information. It seemed pretty obvious that if I didn't show up at two, Sheriff Gibbs wanted to know where he could come looking for me.

I pulled away from the curb and made a slow U-turn. I was uncomfortable. I knew the Sheriff and his deputies would be grabbing at anything they could get their hands on to solve this case. I just didn't want to be among the trees they shook. As I drove away, I noticed an old BMW pull up behind me and follow me down the road. Already antsy, I made a few irrelevant turns on and off Main Street. The BMW stayed with me and then flashed its lights at me. There seemed to be only the driver in the car and the driver appeared to be a female but I knew of too many federal agents and other police types that had made the fatal mistake of underestimating the alleged weaker sex. I pulled back onto Main and stopped at a busy gas station. The BMW pulled up along side of me.

"Hey, thanks for stopping, I'm Sarah Stone," she said as she got out of her car and walked over to me. Ms Stone epitomized the young healthy American female adult of the approaching new millennium. Dressed in tight blue jeans, a white button up shirt, and shiny brown cowboy boots, she had an air of confidence about her. She looked as though she could run a marathon - and probably had, could rope and tie a steer - and probably had, and could ski the roughest black diamond slopes the west had to offer - and probably had. Although the experts most likely wouldn't have called her beautiful, at my age I was getting less critical. Her hair was blond, I had no idea if it was natural or not.   There was nothing about her that was threatening, though, so I got out of my car and shook her extended hand. It was a nice hand.

"I'm a reporter for the Denton Round-up. It's our local paper. I'm trying to get some information on what happened last night. I know the killings occurred but that's about it. I saw you drive up to the Fenster's place and talk to the Sheriff. Would you mind telling me who you are and what your connection with all this is?"

Normally I would shy away from the press. Not really for any reason of distrust or dislike, but simply because in the military we were well trained to refer their inquiries to the Public Affairs Office. It was a system that was easy and smart to stick with. Even with cases that received national attention, I found it convenient and effective to avoid the limelight and the scrutiny. I hadn't really done anything since I retired to get the attention of the press and didn't really think this was a good time to change my ways. However, it was hard for me to shake the feeling that persisted that I might have somehow caused Luke's death, and perhaps because of that, his grandmother's.

"I'm Jim West and I'm not sure if I can be of any help to you Susan. But, if you are willing to buy me a cup of coffee at the diner across the street I'd be willing to discuss what I know, if you don't mind answering a few questions for me."

She didn't even bat an eye. "You're on. And by the way, it's Sarah, not Susan." We crossed the wide road together and entered an old looking cafe that consisted of a nice hardwood bar, a counter lined with stools and a half dozen or so tables covered with blue and white table cloths spread out in the adjacent dining area. Ms. Sarah Stone led me to a table in the far corner. I thought she was overdoing our privacy, especially as there were only two other old men in the entire cafe and they were sitting at the counter by the cafe's entrance.

"Is that James or just Jim? And do you mind if I take notes?" As we sat down, she pulled out a small notepad from her expensive looking leather handbag. Before I could respond an elderly waitress approached us and offered us coffee and a menu. We declined the menu but accepted the coffee.

As the waitress departed, I responded, "It's just Jim. Never been a James and no, I don't mind if you take notes but I really have very little to tell you. I met Luke at a college class while I was guest lecturing last week at a University. He left the class in the middle of my lecture. He never returned. I talked to the professor yesterday, who was also worried about him. As I only live a few miles south of here, he asked if I would come up and check on Luke. Guess I shouldn't have waited until today. Now that's about all I know, so how about if I ask you a few questions?"

"Hold on a minute. I'm paying for the coffee," she said with a smile. "What made Luke walk out of your class?"

"I don't really know, but I do know he appeared upset about something." I didn't want to tell a local reporter about the hypnosis. If I did, I would likely end up on the front page of the local paper. Then I would probably have a more difficult time than ever getting out of town.

She continued to press me for anything more that could help

her with her coverage of the crime but soon realized that I really didn't have any inside scoop to what exactly had happened. At a lull in the conversation, I decided to try again, "Did you know Luke, Ms. Stone?"

This time she wasn't as reluctant, "I knew him but not that well. He was about eight years younger than me. I remember him best from one of the summers when I was in high school. For a short period of time I used to watch him for his grandmother while he played in Smitty's Park. He was getting too old to be under the constant eye of his grandmother and she was getting too old to stay up with him. Somehow, I got drafted to watch him while he played ball or just horsed around with his friends up at the park. She would call me and say that Luke was on his way to the park and ask if I could keep an eye on him for her. If she couldn't get in touch with me, his granny would call some of the other girls until she found one that could. I like to think I was her favorite, but who knows. We all knew her from church. She was the nicest lady." Her voice trailed off as she stared out the big window, trying to fight off the tears.

I felt uncomfortable. Somehow I felt responsible for all this. I didn't know why, and I knew it wasn't anything I had intended or even specifically done. But her tears were like a soft shower, falling on the seeds of guilt already taking root in my soul.

Chapter 3

I pulled up to the Sheriff's office a few minutes early. I liked the architecture being used in so many New Mexico cities and towns these days - the Santa Fe motif, as I refer to it. The current trend in designing court houses, city halls, and other local government offices seemed to be leaning towards revitalizing the old culture. But here in Denton the Sheriff's office had been constructed with adobe several decades ago and already sported the old look. It wasn't a very large building but it was distinctive. I couldn't help but think of how many stories and legends of the Wild West it must have nurtured and witnessed within its walls.

My imagination was interrupted when I noticed one of the sheriff's deputies, whom I thought I had seen earlier that day at Luke's house, staring down at me through the grills of one of the windows facing the main road. I trotted up the few steps to the main entrance no longer day dreaming about the way the west was won.

Once inside, the impressiveness of the building faded quickly. The lobby area had certainly seen better days. The water stained ceiling over the reception counter drew my eyes toward it immediately. Behind the reception counter sat a woman, probably pushing her sixties, in a deputy's uniform who greeted me with a bored smile. "May I help you?" She inquired. I couldn't help but think she looked as worn out as the building. I responded that I was there to see the sheriff, per his invitation, and gave her my name. She pointed out the old wooden benches that lined the wall in the reception area and asked me to have a seat. As I sat down I noticed she had picked up her telephone and seemed to be announcing my arrival to someone. There was no one else on any of the benches, a fact I erroneously assumed to mean that at least I wouldn't have to wait long to be seen.

After staring at the walls, which could all have used a new coat of paint ten years ago, for about thirty minutes, I finally got impatient and re-approached the counter. "Is the sheriff going to be able to see me today? I have a long drive back home."

Looking up from the pocket novel she was reading, she replied, "His secretary said that he was still out of the building, but that he said you were to wait for him here. I don't think he'll be much longer."

Not much longer was about twenty more minutes. I was going to give him thirty and was glad he beat my suspense. I stood up as he walked in. He looked at me briefly and beckoned me with his right hand to follow him down a dark narrow corridor to the rear of the building. I followed him thinking that this was the second person today in Denton that had led me around like this.

We turned into a sunlit room and the sheriff pointed to a comfortable looking, stuffed chair at one end of a coffee table which I took for an invite to sit down. There was no one else in the room. I gave a little sigh of relief as all signs looked as though at least I wasn't suspect number one. The sheriff poured himself a cup of coffee from a small pot in the far corner of the room and looked at me inquisitively, holding the cup up in the air a little. I felt like making a smart comment like "Cat got your tongue", but decided not to, and simply declined. He walked over and slumped into the couch adjacent to the chair I was occupying.

"This has been a terrible day," he started. "I've been sheriff of Sadler County for six years. Before that I was a deputy off and on here in Denton and down in Las Cruces. I've seen other homicides, we aren't perfect up here. It's just this one makes no sense. Who would execute, and that's what it was, not just your run of the mill killing, a granny old enough to die any day now anyway and a young man visiting from college who never caused a lick of trouble his whole life here in town. Nothing was stolen, nothing was broken, there was no evidence of any struggle, no sexual assault, no nothing. The old lady's purse was right next to her body with over a hundred dollars cash in it. My men are trying to lift some prints from the house right now, but I wouldn't bet a plug nickel that we are going to find one that belong to any of the "America's Most Wanted." I assumed he was referring to one of those TV shows on these days, but I guess he could have meant some list the FBI maintained.

"Anyone else live there in the house?"

He shook his head but didn't respond verbally to my question. Rather, he gave me a serious look and said, "Mr. West, I've been checking you out. I was hoping my call down to Curry County would have identified the car you are driving as being stolen or that you were trouble of one sort or another. Anything that would have helped me hang this thing on you.

You are the only thing out of the ordinary I have. Unfortunately everyone down there thinks you walk on water. In fact Sheriff Grant even claims he has learned a thing or two from you and has recommended I try and do the same. Well Mr. West, I don't have time for any lessons telling me how I can do my job better, but if you have any idea who may have killed those two people last night, I am completely open to anything you have to offer."

"I'm sorry Sheriff. I wish I had something substantial I could tell you. I didn't know Luke. I've never been to that house and have never met his grandmother. I just know that in a class I was teaching last week, I reminded him of something that startled him. I don't have the slightest idea what that something was. All I know is that he left the classroom and never returned. Yesterday I talked to the professor, at whose class I was guest lecturing, and told him I would drive up here to see what had bothered Luke and to see if I couldn't talk him into returning to the college. I understood he was a good student. I arrived this morning. After getting coffee and directions to his house, I drove out there. That's when you saw me this morning."

"What was it that set him off?" asked Gibbs.

"I don't really know. It's really kind of odd actually. I make a little extra money giving lectures or leading discussions at universities and at the occasional Lion's Club or Kiwana's. Usually I talk about the use of the polygraph or forensic hypnosis in today's criminal investigations. I enjoy it and the audience doesn't usually complain. Last week I was giving a lecture and Luke volunteered to be my guinea pig in a demonstration for the rest of the class. It was really a simple demonstration. I hypnotized him and took him back in time to see how well he could recall things that happened early in his life. It turned out that Luke was a good choice - sometimes I get people who simply fight the hypnosis or who just like to play games with me. Luke seemed to be exceptionally receptive and his recall was very good. I got him to think back to his second birthday, something I had never been able to do with anyone else, when all of the sudden he started screaming. I brought him out of the trance and sent him out for a drink of water. He did not return to the class and to the best of my knowledge, he left that day and never returned to the university. Dr. Anaya can pretty much verify everything I said."

Sheriff Gibbs and I discussed the possibilities of what Luke could have remembered or thought to have remembered back in his youth, but ultimately decided that guesswork wasn't going to get us anywhere. He told me that he would have to do some research on what may have happened in Luke's early life.

He admitted he was grabbing at straws but that was all he had. None of the neighbors had seen a thing at the scene of the crime and other leads were meager. "Murder is easier to solve in some ways than other crimes," he commented as we walked together back out to the building's front steps, "we can usually determine when it happened, how it happened, and where it happened. Sometimes we can even tell why. It's just the "who" that has to get pinned down. People don't realize that you're a hundred times more likely to get caught if you commit a murder than if you just stick to stealing things." With that sage bit of commentary, to which I felt like responding that it wasn't much help to a victim, we said our good byes and I walked to my car.

I had just about reached it when I heard Gibbs shout my name. I turned and he further ruined my day by saying, "By the way, do me a favor and don't leave town just yet. I may need you. Besides, we have a couple of hotels in town that could do with some business."

I had no desire to stick around in Denton. However, at the same time, I didn't feel like it would be good for me to start irritating the local sheriff. Plus, I still couldn't shake my own sense of responsibility. None of the town's hotels looked too great. I figured they simply provided warmth and security to the wayward traveler who accidentally ended up here, too tired to go as far as was required to get somewhere else. I checked into the Mesa Inn, just next to the place I had breakfast that morning, and smiled as politely as I could when I told the receptionist to give me the best room they had and to charge it to Sheriff Gibb's account. I was surprised she didn't call to verify the Sheriff's generosity, but I guess she wanted to first get me into the hotel and then wrangle out who was going to pay later. I told her I figured on being there no more than two nights.

The room wasn't fancy. Just your basic motel room with a small table and chair, a medium size television, a small couch and what looked to me to be a queen sized bed. The light brown carpet had been worn thin by the entrance. The bathroom also looked as though it needed updating. At least the room's window had a nice view of the street.

I left the room to walk down to a McDonald's that was about

two blocks east of the motel. I didn't know what a vegetarian would do in this town. I originally planned to eat there but decided to just get my meal to go. I walked back to my room and ate the Big Mac while I watched my Braves lose again. It might be a long season. The game wasn't quite over when I turned it off and went to bed.

Again, I tossed and turned all night long. Sleep came on occasion but never stayed for long. I had too many thoughts darting in and out of my mind, and the road outside my window had too many trucks heading somewhere else. I didn't realize it at the time, but I was not the only person in town that night having trouble sleeping.

Chapter 4

Sheriff Gibbs knew better than to try to fight the night. His life had not been an easy one and self-doubts and fears somehow always managed to steal through to his consciousness on nights like this one. Two people had been killed, assassinated right in the middle of his small town and he hadn't the slightest clue who the killer could be. He sat out back of his house on a concrete and brick patio that added little security from the dust and bugs that owned the surrounding fields. Gibbs' fear was rarely for his own physical safety and was never caused by job insecurity. Tough and confident on the outside, only a few who knew him the best, his wife and a few old and close friends, understood his life long obsession with not wanting to let others down. It was not that Gibbs had a history of failing. Nor did it matter that frequently he had made the game winning play for his high school football team, that as a deputy on many occasions he had to do the improbable and unexpected to save a life, and that once he had even delivered a child. He accepted the victories well and moved on. The mistakes of others he could frequently overlook.

It was the fear of failure, the letting down of others who were counting on him that ate away on the inside. As a youth it was the rare fielding error or the fumbled football that he couldn't get over, despite the dozens of great plays that he might have had in the same game. As a professional law enforcement officer, it was the one partner he had lost to a crazy husband who shot the deputy simply because he was there at the time. Thinking they had settled the domestic dispute, Gibbs had just left the room to see who was pounding on the door to the apartment when the husband went berserk and attacked the deputy. Within seconds the guy had shot the deputy and his wife, and then turned the gun on himself. All three died before Gibbs could get them to the hospital. For days Gibbs was physically sick from the anguish over not being there to protect or take the bullet for his partner. He still had the occasional nightmare over it.

Years later he had taken a wrong turn while speeding through a remote part of the county to a house fire. He had only lost three or four minutes before discovering his mistake but was still the first responder to get to the burning home. He burned off half his uniform and blistered much of his face and hands while pulling three small children out of the house. The ambulance arrived just as he was pulling the third child out. The medics and then-deputy Gibbs did all they could to resuscitate the three. Briefly two of the children seemed to respond to the first aid, but eventually all three died enroute to the hospital. All Gibbs could do as he rode along in the back of the ambulance was sit there and watch them die. What really drove the pain to the center of Gibbs soul were comments he overheard at the hospital, that if someone could have only gotten the children out of the smoke a minute or two earlier they might have all survived.

The night the three children died, Gibbs was awake and feverish. Although he confided his feelings of guilt to his wife, he refused to discuss the matter with anyone else. For three days, he stayed home from work. Not as a means of escape but literally because he was in no shape to carry a weapon and do his job. His wife did all she could do to console him but knew only too well that this internal struggle was one that he had to wage alone.

Although these were not the only "mistakes" he had made as an adult, they were the biggest ones. While molding the inner turmoil that arose in Sheriff Gibbs from time to time, they weren't specifically on his mind this night. He sat out and looked at the dark sky hoping to catch a glimpse of a shooting star or even a passing satellite. He couldn't sleep. He only tossed and turned with his thoughts running wild, wondering who else in town might get murdered in the next day or two while he sat impotent in his office. Resisting fatigue until it finally crept up on him near dawn, he counted six satellites and two shooting stars that night.

Chapter 5

I awoke with a start at the ringing of the phone next to the bed. As I reached for the phone I was surprised to see that it was nearly eight in the morning. I usually wake up earlier but my fitful night of sleep must have affected my internal alarm clock, too. After I mumbled out a hello, I received my second surprise of the morning when I heard Ms. Stone's voice on the line.

"This is Sarah. What are you doing for breakfast? I've got some news for you."

"What is it?"

"No way, I get some free coffee for this. Meet me in the Pancake House in fifteen minutes." With that she hung up. I sat on the bed for a minute trying to figure out how she knew I was still in town, where I was staying, and finally what news she could have for me this early in the morning.

It took me twenty minutes to get cleaned up, shaved and to the restaurant. Fortunately the hotel had some complimentary razors and tooth brushes, but I still felt dingy in the same outfit I had worn the day before. I started to think it wasn't just the local hotel business Sheriff Gibbs was trying to support. If I had to stay another day I would certainly have to buy a change of clothes.

Ms. Stone was already at a table. She had a large stack of pancakes and a pot of coffee in front of her.

"I thought you just said coffee," I said with a smile as I sat down. Meeting women for breakfast was not something I was used to anymore and despite everything going on, all of a sudden I felt pretty good.

"I'll pay for the pancakes," she said returning the smile. "I shouldn't be eating them any way. It's not easy to keep one's weight down."

I hoped she didn't notice my waist suddenly being sucked in an inch or two. I told the waitress I'd have the same as Ms. Stone.

"Sorry if I woke you up, I talked to Sheriff Gibbs this morning. He told me he asked you to stay in town. We discussed your comments about something scaring Luke, something that he remembered about his second birthday. Although I personally find that a little far fetched, you may be interested in knowing that on Luke's second birthday a neighbor of his, a Mrs. Annie Shell was murdered. She was baby-sitting Luke and was discovered by Luke's mother when she came over to the house to pick him up. Luke was found in the same room with Mrs. Shell. He was not hurt, but that's all I know about how the incident affected him. Anyway, that may be what he remembered, if a person could really recall what happened on their second birthday. Me, I can't remember anything before age six or seven. But it doesn't seem to help us much in this case."

"Did they find the murderer?" For whatever reason, I wasn't going to let go of this lead so easily.

"Yes, someone had seen a stranger in town, acting suspiciously and hanging around the neighborhood. When the

Sheriff, it wasn't Sheriff Gibbs back then, tried to arrest him, he took off running and was hit by a truck as he tried to cross the main highway. He died before the Sheriff was able to get a statement from him, but he had Mrs. Shell's wallet in a small back pack he was carrying."

"Well, it certainly could explain why I got such a reaction out of Luke. And, while it unfortunately doesn't help out much in solving his murder, I guess it means there is no longer a need for me to stay in town." After I said it, I felt kind of funny, comparing Luke's death and the town's mystery with my own desire to go home. I started to say I didn't really mean it the way it sounded, when a young man in brown slacks and a bright yellow shirt walked up to the table.

"So, Sarah, this is your mystery man." He gave Sarah a wink and then turned to me, "I'm Rick Jimenez, the other reporter for the Denton paper."

I said hello.

With a mischievous smile he turned back to Sarah, "After our conversation this morning, I did some more homework. I am not too sure the man they think killed Annie Shell was really the murderer. I am working on a theory of my own. Anyways, just wanted to let you know. Enjoy your breakfast." With that he turned to walk off.

"What do you mean by that?" I asked, but he just looked back at Sarah and winked again.

"Don't let him bother you. He's a little strange but he's actually a nice guy," she said in his defense.

"Are you two a couple?"

She shook her head, still grinning. "No. We have dated a

few times, but our chemistry is so different, it couldn't work."

I called the waitress over and asked for the entire check. I was surprised Sarah didn't protest. But then I already knew that I would never be an expert on women. I thanked her for her company and said that I thought I might be leaving town later that day but that if I ever made it back up to Denton, I might look her up. She nodded, grabbed my hand, leaned over and kissed me on my cheek. She then walked off, looking back with a wink. Odd town I thought, but I also noticed that my heart was racing a little more than normal. The thought of getting back to the safety of my own home was comforting.

I went back into the lobby of the hotel and proceeded to checkout. Despite my comments the night before, I went ahead and paid for the room myself. One night at forty eight dollars, I could handle that.

After packing everything I had that I was not wearing into one small plastic bag, I jumped into my car and drove to the Sheriff's office to say my good-byes. Unfortunately, when I arrived at the Sheriff's office I found out that the Sheriff had gone to Santa Fe and would not be back until mid-afternoon and had left a note for me to see him around three in the afternoon. I was irritated but I figured it would still give me time to get home before dark.

I decided to drive to Lake Conchas, about thirty miles northwest of town, to kill some time. I had often thought of buying some property overlooking the lake but had never gotten around to it. In fact, I hadn't been to the lake in a couple of years, so I thought it might be interesting to see what was even available these days.

It was another clear day and the drive up was scenic and relaxing. Easy by car but I couldn't help thinking how rugged the country must have been for anyone traveling through it a hundred years ago. For all the stories about the dangers from the Indians, I imagine just finding food and water was the bigger problem. It could get really hot in New Mexico in the summer and, for that matter, really cold in the winter. One could easily see why there were so many deserted towns and houses scattered through the country side. Give me the twentieth century any day.

Conchas Lake was one of the largest in New Mexico. Trapping the runoff from the mountains behind a large dam, it turned the southern half of the Canadian River into nothing more than a creek. The lake extended about seven miles west of the dam which had widened the river for about four miles north of the lake. Not a popular fishing lake, it was never crowded and perfect for the occasional water skier or jet-ski enthusiast. As a teenager I used to dive off the rock cliffs that lined the north fork of the lake.

I had moved away from New Mexico after high school and although I had passed through the state on a few occasions I had not spent any real time here until my recent move back. I had left a lean, wiry young man full of dreams and ambition and had somehow lost a lot of them in the last decade or two. I didn't think I had become negative in my outlook, just practical. My career had opened my eyes to the evils in the world. I had seen the harsh reality of what one person would do to another and how most people would rather look away, not wanting to get involved when others are threatened.

Somewhere along the way I had lost that lean, wiry physique, too. I didn't consider myself over weight. I had just let myself get out of shape. But I still had all my teeth, plenty of hair on my head and hadn't shrunk from my six foot frame. I thought it could be worse.

Perhaps the biggest change was deeper inside. My wife of fifteen years had walked out on me not too long ago. The hurt was still stifling. She had said that she just wasn't happy anymore, that I had focused too much on my job and too little on her. Three days after her announcement she was gone. I tried talking and then writing but she was gone. I did not think there was anyone else but that didn't make it easier. I knew it was best not to dwell on it.

My search for real estate at the lake would not be hard. There was only one real estate office. A small old wooden structure, the real estate agency obviously wasn't interested in impressing anyone. The agent was out but a hand written note on the door said he would be back in thirty minutes. I noticed that the note was signed off at nine in the morning and as it was now almost eleven, I started to doubt if it was even written today. Another handwritten notice behind some plexi-glass advertised two empty lots for sale. The notice included a brief map, also hand drawn that indicated where the lots were. Although it appeared they were both in an old small residential development I had actually checked out a few years earlier, I decided to take another look.

Taking the only paved road that circled this part of the lake, I was impressed with the wide open beauty of the area. It always amazed me how people could live together so crowded in so many parts of the country. They would pay fortunes for crowded, country lake estates or for vacations at those same lakes, but fail to settle or populate the hundreds of beautiful big lakes in the stretch between New Mexico and Arizona up to Montana. I knew the Ted Turners of the world had begun buying up a lot of the real estate in New Mexico, and for that matter in Montana, but that still didn't explain why the common man hadn't followed suit.

I found the two lots where I thought they would be, in a small concentration of cabins and double-wide trailers. While the lots provided a nice view of the lake, they suffered from the same affliction that the other lots had already accepted – a hastily thrown together segment of real estate, put together by a developer that had no real sense of how to take advantage of the beauty of the lake. The lots were small and the roads once inside the development were narrow and still not paved. All right, I guessed for the middle class business man that liked to pop in for the weekend, or the retiree just wanting to relax. I wasn't that retired.

For a diversion I started to drive further north along the lake's edge, but I soon passed the point where the lake could be seen and started to feel that the road might continue on for a few more miles before it just ended. There seemed to be no sign of human life in the surrounding country. I was looking for a place to turn around when I saw what appeared to be another road running into the one I was on. There was even a sign warning traffic of the upcoming intersection. I chuckled to myself thinking that probably no more than a handful of people had ever even driven on the road I was on, much less the small road approaching from the east. I slowed down to make my u-turn at the intersection when I noticed a man made sign, nothing more than a piece of plywood hammered onto a wooden stake, pointing east with the words Denton and thirty-two miles painted on it.

Feeling a little absurd, I sat there in my car for a few minutes looking at the sign and debating whether I should take advantage of this opportunity. What was silly about the whole thing was that I was actually feeling a little frightened. I wasn't sure if it was just the stark solitude of my situation or what, but I couldn't shake a sense of apprehension. Finally, with a feeling that I wasn't going to be pushed around by some illogical fear, I took the fork to the east. I checked my odometer and figured in thirty three miles if I didn't run into Denton, I'd turn around and make the long drive back to Denton the way I had come. It was still early and I knew there would be nothing to do until mid-afternoon anyway.

The road was narrow and not marked with a center line. But it was straight and other than an occasional small incline, was fairly flat. I thought I could see for about five miles down the road, ample time to get out of way of any oncoming traffic. I also thought that the likelihood of running into any type of speed trap was about zero, so I stepped down a little on the gas, holding the old Ford Probe at eighty five miles per hour.

Whatever had caused my irrational apprehension had dissipated, as a feeling of being free and content settled in. The country side rushed by and I started to think that I would be back in Denton in no time at all. I was even considering whether I should check to see if Ms. Stone, probably time for me to start thinking of her as Sarah, was available for lunch.

After about twenty seven miles in about twenty minutes, I started to look for signs of Denton. Suddenly, a bright flash of sun reflecting off of something several yards off the road hit me square in the eyes. I reacted by touching the brakes and turning my head away from the light, although it had already gone. Unfortunately, in the split seconds of all this I let the car get to the edge of the road and to what normally would be a shoulder on most highways in the United States. As it was, my right tires hit a large, jagged pot hole jarring the car and instantly both tires blew. I cursed myself. While I had only reacted nominally to the bright flash, that was all that was needed on this small road. I had to fight to not lose control of the car. Fortunately I was able to safely slow the car and finally brought it to a stop in about a quarter mile.

I got out of my car and walked around to inspect the damage. Other than the two flats the car was undamaged. Unfortunately, I only had one spare. I felt like kicking the car, but I had owned it too long and it was more the road's fault anyway. I contemplated changing one of the tires and then just driving slowly into town with one still flat. I knew it would just do additional damage to the wheel, but I didn't know what other options I really had. Standing there wishing I hadn't even taken this back road "shortcut" to Denton, I looked to see what caused the flash of light. I was fairly certain it had been the reflection of the sun off something but I couldn't see anything from where I was on the road. I began walking back to see what I had hit, I knew it was either a nasty pot hole or a section of the edge of the road that was eroded away.

I never made it all the way back to the point where the damaged occurred. About fifty yards shy of where I thought the tires had blown I noticed a set of what seemed to be fairly fresh car tracks veering from the road. My first instinct was that someone else had been victimized by the same pot hole that I hit. I followed the tracks a dozen or so yards, mainly out of curiosity. The tracks seemed clean and distinct. There was no indication that the driver had tried to steer the car back onto the road. Although the tracks became hard to see on the hard packed dirt, the damage that the car had done to the light brush helped guide me the next twenty or so yards. I was just beginning to think that I ought to head back up onto the road as I hadn't even locked up my car, when I saw the rear end of a white Suburban sticking up out of a small ravine.

I stood there for a few moments. I dreaded going to check what might be in the car, but at the same time knew I had no choice. I shouted first to see if anyone would answer. Of course, no one did, so I jogged over to the Suburban. The driver's door was open. A good sign, I thought. It obviously meant someone was alive enough to open it. I walked up to look in. The first thing that registered was that no one was there. My relief was short-lived as I quickly realized the red color splattered all over the seat and steering wheel had to be blood. Seeing blood doesn't bother me, I had seen it many times before, but something about being alone in the middle of nowhere with the top half of my body inside the empty interior of a bloody Suburban gave me the creeps. I instinctively pulled my head out and slammed the door. I knew it was a mistake as soon as I did it. First rule of evidence, don't disturb the crime scene. A little thing, but I felt like a rookie. I shouldn't have closed the door. I was beginning to think I wasn't in charge.

I took a few breaths and looked out over the front hood of the car, down the ravine and up the other side. No indication of movement anywhere. The Suburban looked ok from what I could see. I turned around, maybe to head back, maybe to look around. I did neither immediately. I gasped. There just fifteen feet from where I was standing sat Rick Jimenez, the other reporter, as he had described himself that morning, for the town's newspaper. His face was contorted, covered with dried blood, his shirt completely soaked in blood now drying in the sun. He was dead. It took a lot of self discipline to stay put and not start running away.

The noise of the flies now registered in my mind. They should have signaled something in my mind earlier. A few were having a field day around his head. The rest were focused on his shirt. I could see the trail of blood that ran from the car to where Rick had managed to get to the large boulder where he just sat down to rest against it. He must have been trying to get back to the road. He didn't get far. I took a closer look at him. The car accident couldn't have caused those injuries, but it was impossible to tell what did without a real inspection and I wasn't about to break the rules again. My best move was to get to a phone to call the police. I imagined this was all part of Sheriff Gibbs' jurisdiction. But getting to a phone was not going to be that easy.

Chapter 6

I walked back to my car and cursed myself for not having a cell phone. Every body had one these days. I simply did not want to be tied down to phones or beepers, not any more. Just now, however, I was not at all sure my alleged independence was such a smart idea. I had had this internal argument before and I knew I would probably have to conform to the rest of the world and get one some day. But later wasn't going to do me any good today.

It could be hours before another car might come along the old road I was on. I decided to change out the flat front tire with the spare and had just about finished when I heard a car approaching from the direction I had been driving. I stood out in the road and waved at the approaching car which turned out to be a Ford pick-up. It was driven by a young man and a second person was in the passenger seat. They braked the pick-up harder than they really needed to, which proceeded to blow up a lot of dust mostly on my car and me.

When the dust settled, I could see them both smiling out at me. I could only imagine the dust "explosion" they created had given them great satisfaction. The passenger, another young man, leaned out his window.

"What's up Mister, do you need a hand?" I figured they both could still be in their late teens, possibly early twenties at the oldest.

"There has been an accident down there," I pointed back to where the Suburban was stranded. "Could you all drive into town and send the Sheriff out here?"

"What for? We could just tow it out. The Sheriff would just tell us to pull it out. Where is it? I can't see it. Where's the driver?" I could see the passenger wasn't use to calling anyone for help.

The driver got out of the pick-up and walked around to me. "Did he hit your car? It doesn't look too bad. Do you want us to tow you into Denton?" They obviously wanted to tow someone, somewhere.

I could see I was getting nowhere. "The driver of the Suburban is dead. I believe he is Rick Jimenez from the paper. And, I don't think it was the accident that killed him. I think someone shot him." The two young men stared at me. I had gotten their attention. "I need you to go into town and get the Sheriff."

"Why don't we just call him?" asked the driver. They both reached into their pockets and each produced a small cell phone. Despite the seriousness of the moment, I couldn't help but internally be amused at how the world had changed. One of them, the driver, who I later learned was Dave Hepp, quickly dialed 911 and was patched through to the Sheriff's office. He relayed that there was an emergency, that a person was dead. He further identified the road we were on as Old Creek Road and our location as four miles northeast of town. He obviously was from the area, as I had yet to see a sign indicating how close we were to Denton or the name of the road.

Dave's passenger was Saul Church. Despite their curiosity, I was able to convince both of them to stay with me and not hike back to look at the dead body. I offered to take them when the Sheriff showed up. They helped me finish replacing the one flat tire. I learned that the two had graduated from high school the year before and decided to work a year on one of the nearby ranches prior to starting college. They seemed like good kids and I encouraged them to go to college when they finished the year. I knew if they waited too long they may never go.

Like so many young men, and in particular those from this part of the country, this was the age that they truly felt like they ruled the world. They were out of high school and working odd jobs on a number of ranches. The work was fun. To them, the money they were making was a fortune. Although most still lived at home, they were more independent than ever before and loved it.

In less than ten minutes we could see a Sheriff's car and an ambulance racing up the road towards us. A second Sheriff's car was soon in view about a mile behind the first. When the first of the two vehicles pulled up next to us, a deputy jumped out. I had the impression that after surveying the three of us and lack of damage that the deputy initially thought that we may have played a prank in getting them to respond.

"What the hell is going on? Did you all call in an accident?" He was the deputy who first talked to me in front of Luke's house and seemed to be addressing his questions to me, and not with much patience.

"We called it in, officer, but the victim is down there in the gully." I turned and pointed in the general direction.

"I don't see anything," he grunted.

I was beginning to think if Sheriff Gibbs didn't have any better talent than this to support him, that he may never solve the two, now possibly three murders in his county. I had already come up with my own theory that this death had to be related to the other two.

Fortunately, when the other car arrived Sheriff Gibbs hopped out. He looked at me warily and motioned for his deputy to come back to him. I could hear the deputy telling Gibbs what I had told him. Gibbs walked up to me.

"Take me to what you saw" was all that he said. As the whole crowd of us started walking off the road in the direction of the Suburban, he suddenly stopped and turned around. "Hey come on, not everyone." Then for whatever reason, he changed his mind. "Okay, you all can come but stay about ten paces behind Mr. West and me and watch where you are walking. Let me know if you see anything at all out of the ordinary." He turned to me and softly commented that the two "boys", as he referred to them, were sharper than any of his deputies any way and could probably help search the area around the body. "He is dead, right?" he asked and after I nodded he commented that he certainly didn't want to be taking his time if there was any chance to save the person.

When we got near the body I purposely took him around the crime scene to a point farthest from the road and to an area I had not disturbed. I chose a point where both the car and the body could easily be seen, as well as the tracks leading away from the car back up towards the road.

I explained to the Sheriff how I had been driving down the road and how on the bend I was momentarily blinded by a reflection of sunlight. This bright flash caused me to let the right tires get too close to the edge of the road. The jagged broken edges of the road did the rest, tearing a gash in both tires on the right side of my car. Stranded, I had decided to walk back to see what caused the reflection. I discovered the Suburban. I admitted that I had touched the car as I had not known about the body until after looking inside the car.

I was impressed with his patience in letting me get through my entire story before he asked any questions. "That's Jimenez, isn't it?" He asked of his deputy. The group had inched up to a few feet behind us as I was telling my story to the Sheriff. Their approach had not seemed to bother the Sheriff. "Did any one bring a camera?" He asked his deputy and the medical personnel.

"I did," beamed his deputy.

"Where is it?" Gibbs asked.

"In the car."

"Then go get it, and follow your same tracks, both ways. And radio back for more help."

"Yes, sir" responded the deputy as he rushed back towards the road.

While the deputy was gone, Sheriff Gibbs stood still looking at the crime scene. I didn't know what was going through his mind. I imagine he was just trying to draw something out of the scene that would later help him solve the case. I knew some investigators would spend hours after a crime scene search going over photos taken at the scene in an attempt to see something previously over looked. Although I did not really want to interrupt his thinking, I felt obligated to comment on the events earlier in the day.

"I know you may not want to hear this, Sheriff, but I believe this killing may be related to the other two." He turned his attention towards me, without commenting. "This morning I was having breakfast with Ms. Stone, from the paper, when this gentlemen" I nodded towards the dead body, "came by and remarked to Ms. Stone that he had a theory on the killings. He made some comment that the killings may be related to the murder that happened back on Luke's second birthday. For whatever reason he did not seem to think that the person blamed for that earlier murder was really responsible for it. I think whatever lead he was pursuing got him too close to the murderer."

"Did he or Sarah give you any indications as to whom or what he was specifically talking about?"

"No, and I don't think Sarah had any idea either. But you should probably talk to her, too."

We stayed out at the site where the body was discovered until dark. Both the Sheriff and I were fairly certain that the actual crime did not occur there. How exactly Jimenez managed to drive himself consciously or unconsciously was beyond us, but there was absolutely no indication of any other person being in the car or in the immediate vicinity of the Suburban. There was considerable blood in the Suburban; not only in the driver's seat but also some on the passenger seat where it looked like Jimenez had placed a handkerchief that he had been using to try to stop his bleeding. Blood had dripped on the console and some had even gathered on the floor just behind the front seats. Nothing had smeared the blood on the passenger seat or on the floor. The quantity of blood on the driver's seat made it obvious that Jimenez had been in the vehicle for some time after being shot.

After what seemed to be hundreds of photographs taken of the scene, the emergency medical personnel took a close-up, cursory review of the body. Under the caked blood, an entrance wound of a bullet could be seen above the left eye. The sheriff, taking no chances, told them to carefully bag the body to minimize the possibility of any fiber or other evidence from falling off. A more detailed exam of the clothing could be done at the state lab and the coroner would have plenty of time to thoroughly analyze the body.

"He couldn't have driven very far in his condition." I surmised, speaking softly to the Sheriff. "It's amazing the bullet wound didn't kill him immediately. The only thing I can think is that the bullet was deflected slightly as it hit bone and scooted around just inside the skull."

"You're probably right. The sad thing is if he just kept his car on the road someone may have found him in time to save him or at least find out who shot him."

Both Dave and Saul proved to be as hard working as the Sheriff had predicted. After getting over the initial shock of seeing the body, they were sent to search a swath of land ten yards on either side of the tracks left by the Suburban all the way back to the road. The sheriff gave them each a pair of protective gloves that he told them to wear and a box of quart size zip lock bags, instructing them to put anything they found that could have been dropped or fallen off a person into individual bags. They were told to document where they found the item on a sheet of paper and scotch tape the sheet to the outside of the bag. If they saw anything that looked like a weapon or had blood on it they were not to touch it, but to call back to the sheriff. Neither the Sheriff nor I thought they would find anything significant, perhaps nothing at all.

By the time we were getting ready to leave, they had actually found twenty four separate items that they had bagged. Unfortunately, nothing appeared to be significant. Most of what they had bagged were cigarette butts and cans that had been thrown from passing cars over the previous months or years. But one certainly had to give them credit for their effort. The Sheriff offered to buy them dinner for their help but both said they would take a rain check as their parents would most certainly be looking forward to their getting home and hearing of the day's adventures

A tow truck came and took the Suburban back to town. As the first of the night's stars started breaking through the darkening sky, I sat on the front hood of my car and tried to make sense of the day's discovery with Sheriff Gibbs. Despite his calm handling of the search process, I could sense that the stress of the past couple of days was getting to him. This was slightly troubling as I had been consistently impressed with his handling of the investigation to date.

"What do you think is going on?" I asked, hoping to get him to open up to what was bothering him.

"I don't know but we need to start getting some breaks. Tomorrow, I'll have a couple of the guys check up and down the road and perhaps a couple of the side roads to see if we can determine where the shooting took place."

"Good idea. Maybe forensics will be able to put something together that can link these crimes and perhaps even point us to someone."

"I have no doubt that they are linked. Unfortunately, I also have no doubt the killer is someone from the local area, someone we all know. For the life of me though I can't figure out a motive, nor can I picture anyone in this community doing this. I know people change, have hidden personalities, and all that, it is just hard to picture someone I know doing anything like this."

"You certainly don't know everyone in a fifty mile radius, do you?" I intended my comment to be as much of a statement as a question.

"No, not all of them, but most. You need to realize that new people very rarely move into Denton. We are not a big draw to the common American. Don't get me wrong, I like it here, it's beautiful and the people are great. Well, most are. But our population probably hasn't changed by more than a handful in the past twenty years."

"How about those out in the county, away from the city?"

"Same thing, I know most of them. There are a few though that keep to themselves, but most are so connected to Denton for their banking, schooling, or whatever, that I know them as well as the city folk. The ones that keep to themselves, mostly the older ones, have never caused me any problem." He looked at me, smiled and said, "Heck, you were the closest thing to a good suspect that has showed up around here for some time. And, if you keep stumbling upon crime scenes, you may just move back into that category."

He was smiling, but I didn't care for the comment. I had already realized the bad habit I was developing of showing up at the wrong place at the wrong time. There were hundreds of Sheriffs in the country that would have locked me up by now if elections were looming. Fortunately, I didn't think Gibbs fit this category. More fortunately, perhaps, it wasn't election season.

I didn't think Sheriff Gibbs had actually touched on what was bothering him in the conversation we just had. I figured it was something deeply seeded, but the arrival of a second tow truck stopped our conversation.

I was amazed by the old man that got out of the tow truck. He looked to be at least eighty. I was more impressed however by his agility in hooking up my car in the dwindling daylight. Sheriff Gibbs comments were brought home as I noticed the logo on the side of his truck referred to forty years of service to the Denton area.

I jumped into the Sheriff's car and we followed the tow truck into Denton. "Old Max has been in the towing and repair business for as long as I can remember. I first met him when my car broke down on this same road when I was in high school. He's a good worker and pleasant enough fellow. No wonder his business is a success."

When we arrived back in town the Sheriff dropped me off at Max's garage. Despite the late hour, Max had said he could have my car ready in just a few minutes. He had tires that matched the ones that were blown and simply wouldn't hear of me going the evening without my car. Once again, I had the pleasure of watching this old man as he quickly and methodically replaced the two tires. I offered to help but he mumbled something about insurance and declined my assistance. Max struck me as the same type of person who settled in and developed this rugged section of the country a century earlier.

"How long have you lived here, Max?" I had to ask.

"All my life," was his answer.

"Were your folks here all their lives, too?"

He looked over at me, I guess trying to figure out why I was asking. "My mother was born on a ranch over by the Texas border. My father was with the railroad. He was actually from St. Louis, but settled here after meeting my Mom."

He didn't offer anything else and I decided not to keep pressing him. I had a natural fascination with life in the old southwest. It had to have been a very rough existence. I always enjoy reading and hearing stories about life back then.

Within the hour I was back out on the city streets driving my car. As I passed a branch office of Century 21 Real Estate, lit up by a flood light, I couldn't help but wonder just how long my stay in Denton was going to be.

When I returned to the hotel, I had a couple of surprises waiting for me. First, the hotel had already gotten word to hold my room for another night, and secondly, the receptionist handed me a note from Sarah to give her a call. I considered calling her right away, but quickly realized that I was too tired and hungry to do much more than grab a quick bite and turn in for the evening. It had certainly been a long day. I called down to the front desk to see if they could deliver a sandwich from the pancake house next door. I was pleased to hear the "no problem" reply. I jumped into the shower and emerged just in time to answer the room service knock at the door.

The same receptionist who had checked me back in was standing there with the sandwich in hand. I thanked her and paid her for the sandwich and her service, but before I could close the door, she asked, "Did you call her?"

"Who?" I responded, momentarily forgetting about the note I had been given to call Sarah.

"Sarah, I gave you a note from her."

"I thought that note was for me. How did you know what it said?"

"She wrote it at the counter and discussed it with me. I've known Sarah for a long time."

"Well, I'll call her in the morning. It's been a long day, it's getting late, and I need to crash."

"Okay," she responded, "you know Sarah is a real sweet girl. You could do a lot worse." With that she winked, turned around and walked away.

Winking must be a fad in this town, I thought, more stuck at the moment with the wink than the comments. It wasn't until after I had eaten the sandwich and was lying in bed that her comments sunk in. I couldn't imagine what motivated her to make the remark but dwelling on it helped bring about a pleasant night's sleep.

Chapter 7

For the second morning in a row, the phone rang at eight. Due to the coincidence, I was not surprised when the caller turned out to be Ms. Stone.

"How about another round of pancakes?" she asked.

My feelings were mixed. On the one hand I was irritated by the call disrupting my sleep, on the other I was starting to enjoy the sound of her voice. Without much internal debate, I heard myself answer, "Okay, same place as yesterday?"

"I'm already there," she replied confidently.

As I hung up the phone, the unpleasant reality of putting on the same clothes that I had already worn for a couple of days hit me. I would have to buy some additional clothing, and soon, but to do so I had to get dressed again in the dirty, wrinkled ones.

I felt a little self-conscious walking back in to the restaurant looking more like a bum than I liked. But if anyone noticed, nobody said anything.

I found Sarah at the same table she had been a day earlier. This time however, she did not appear to be her same perky self. She tried to put on a happy front as I joined her but it was easy to tell that, understandably, the death the day before of her good friend was bothering her. We passed a few comments back and forth about the day and the weather. I even made a hurried apology for my clothes, but she quickly got to the point.

"What's going on?" she asked, "Who would want to kill Ricky? He hasn't got," she caught herself, "didn't have an enemy in the world."

"Too frequently there is little logic and no fairness in this world of ours. Those are traits we try to create and maintain. Too often things happen that don't make sense and certainly are unfair. The jobs of people like Sheriff Gibbs are needed at times like this to bring things back to what we perceive as the norm. It falls on them to track down individuals with deviant behavior and to bring those people to justice."

We sat and theorized about what may have happened. Mostly, I just tried to let Sarah vent. Despite her denials the day before, she and Rick Jimenez must have had a fairly close and long term friendship. They had been working together for a while and as the only two journalists in their age group they had bonded quite well, despite the friendly competition to scoop one another. Most of the writers for the paper were older and the editor often referred to them both as the future of the paper. A concept both were content with and had come to accept.

We sat there for over an hour. I found myself surprisingly hungry and ate my entire breakfast. Sarah, on the other hand, only nibbled hers. The restaurant was not very busy and the wait staff was patient with us. Small towns, I thought as Sarah talked about Rick, often took on the personality of an extended family in times of crises. The employees of the restaurant did seem to understand the suffering that Sarah was experiencing.

Finally, she was quiet for a moment looking at her coffee. When she looked up, she asked, "What's next?"

I wasn't sure what she meant and told her so.

"I mean, what's next - what is the killer going to do next and what are we going to do to catch him?"

"Slow down, Sarah, you are making too many assumptions. First, we don't know if the person who killed Rick also killed Luke and his Grandmother. Nor is there any reason to think that 'We' are going to do anything about it. The Sheriff is in charge of this investigation and if you ask me, he is one smart fellow. Whoever the murderer is, I think his days of walking the streets in public are numbered."

"I thought all night about what has happened in this town the last few days," she continued, impervious to what I thought was fairly sound logic, "the killer has to be one and the same. Rick made that comment to us yesterday morning, you remember it. I thought at the time he had a lead on the killing, but I never would have guessed he would have followed up on it to the extent that he must have. I think he must have confronted the killer."

"I don't think Rick would have done that, not if he had any sense at all, and from what I understand he was a bright young man."

"He wouldn't have, unless he ended up face to face with the killer, before he realized who he was. He might have then. Rick was smart but if cornered he would confront and challenge the killer. Dumb male ego - he wouldn't have made up some lame excuse and tried to escape without a confrontation."

"Possible," I admitted, "but you are making another assumption. Why do you think the killer is a man?"

"If it was a woman, it would make Rick's mistake of letting

himself get drawn in too close to the killer more understandable." She paused again for a minute. "The reason we need to do something about it is because if the killer thinks that Rick passed his theory on to anyone it would be me. We have a close working relationship, we're, we were," she said, catching herself again, "friends. It would be a logical assumption. If the killer murdered Rick for what he knew, or what he theorized, I think I might be his next target. For that matter, everyone in town knows that you and I have been together a lot since you have been in town. In fact, outside of the Sheriff, I am about the only other person you have probably spent any time with, so you could be a target too."

I nearly interrupted her to say that I had had a nice conversation with Old Max the night before at the garage, but I didn't think she would enjoy my levity at this moment.

"The Sheriff is a good man," she continued, "but I certainly don't expect him to be my body guard until the killer is in jail. I don't see how you can leave town. You are more linked to the three murders than anyone else I know. I don't mean that as an accusation." She stated, noting my eyebrows going up at her statement. "I just mean that you are a critical witness. You are tied to this case at the hip. I don't think the Sheriff would let you leave town. Nor do I think you would want to at this point."

I knew she had a point. In fact, I had pretty well settled in my own mind the night before that I was going to be in town a lot longer than I had ever planned. I made a mental note to call my neighbor and have them check on Chubs until I could get home.

"I know you are pretty good about these things. The Sheriff's office isn't the only one in town that can do background checks. Our paper also had you checked out the first day you were in town. I'd much rather work with you to find out what is going on, than to do so on my own. But, either way, I am not going to just hide in my home and at the office until the killer is brought to justice. I plan on doing my own digging and would rather have your help than do it alone. What do you say?"

The biggest portion of my common sense was telling me that "working with her" as she put it, would not be the smartest thing to do. It wasn't that I hadn't thought about doing some digging of my own. I had already decided I had been forced into that corner. It was just that I knew I would be better off on my own. Keeping an eye on her would slow me down and definitely be a distraction. But at the same time, her eyes were growing on me and I couldn't help but feel that as a distraction I could do a lot worse. Besides it might be harder to stay away from her than not in this small town, especially if she kept calling me every morning.

"You know, this is not going to be easy," I said. Her smile at me at that moment, knowing that I had just agreed to her proposal, hit me hard. On the one hand, I couldn't help thinking how beautiful she was. On the other, the hair on the back of my neck was telling me that I may actually be starting the process that could lead her, or both of us, to death's front door.

Chapter 8

The old pick-up truck slowed down as it drove by the small house on the corner of Second Street and Joshua. The driver stared out the window at the well kept yard and the red brick, single story residence that occupied it. Sarah had bought the house a year earlier in a step that she thought formalized her personal rise to independence and adulthood. Besides that, she loved the house and was tired of living in the only apartment complex in town.

Unfortunately for Sarah, her theory that the murderer, if he thought Rick had confided in anyone, would jump to Sarah as the likely recipient was right on target. It wasn't that Rick had said anything about sharing his ideas with anyone before he was killed. It was just that Bill White had already lived a life of paranoia far too long to really believe that Rick had taken his theory to the grave with him.

Bill was not worried about anyone seeing him drive by the house. He knew no one would notice him. The absolute confidence that Bill had about his ability to get away with crime, all sorts of crime, had been honed by two decades of being able to avoid prosecution and in most cases even arrest. Killing three people in the span of a few days, however, was an apogee in his bizarre life of crime, and even Bill was having a hard time controlling all the voices in his head. He had gotten little sleep the night before as he hid in the field beside his house watching to see if the police would come for him. If they had, he would have faded off in the night to start life somewhere else. The fact that they didn't gave him some time to clean up a couple of possible leads to his capture. Sarah was one of them and he didn't intend to let her start putting things together as Rick Jemenez had.

Bill's mind, and for that matter his entire life, would have amazed and fascinated even the most experienced criminal psychologists. He not only had many of the classic behavior patterns of a serial killer, he had been officially declared dead years before and had twice assumed the identity of one of his victims.

His current identity fit him especially well and the small ranch just north of Denton lent him the privacy and freedom that he relished. Bill had been living on the ranch for three years and no one, until the old lady and now Jemenez, had realized who he really was.

The old lady had surprised him. She had encountered him in the small grocery store and had even grabbed his arm. "I know you, don't I?" She first asked but then continued. "You grew up here. I don't recall your name, what is it?" Bill had pulled away and started to leave the store but she followed.

"And why are you trying to hide your real appearance?" She had whispered to him almost conspiratorially.

Bill tried to conceal his shock and hurried out of the store leaving his items in the cart he abandoned at the door. She did not follow him out. How could this old woman have seen through his disguise? Worse yet did she know who he really was? He did not think so or she certainly would have called him by name. But she was obviously a threat and one that needed quick attention, yet he knew he couldn't do anything in the store. He instantly decided that he would have to follow her, find out where she lived and then come up with a plan to get rid of her.

Rick Jimenez, on the other hand, hadn't really figured out who White was and posed no threat until he stopped him while he was driving down the road. White had been caught off guard as Jimenez explained to him he had been looking for him and had just come from his house. Rick had told him that he wanted to interview him about reports that a younger man had been seen at his house.

Despite the fact that Bill White had grown up in Denton and was actually only thirty-eight years old, he thought he had been very careful hiding his true appearance. To anyone who saw him, or to the few who came to slightly know him, he was an elderly widower on a pension who had purchased a small ranch north of town and lived a somewhat hermit-like existence. A wig and a little make-up could do magic with one's age.

One could debate whether William Thomas White was born evil or was a product of years of neglect and abuse. But by the time he turned nineteen, he had already committed a wide variety of crimes culminating with the brutal killing of Annie Shell. That murder, spurred by jealousy, whetted his appetite for future slayings. Bill relished in the sense of absolute power that he had over his victims as they fruitlessly struggled, dying in his presence. It was a sensation stronger and more satisfying than anything else he had ever experienced, more potent than drugs and even better than sex. In his warped mind, Bill often imagined that he must be a Highlander, like the characters in the movies and on television, who absorbed the souls of those they killed.

Killing Annie Shell was not something that Bill had planned to do. He knew her most of his teenage years, as she was just three years older than he was, and had spent almost that entire period in love with her. It was not a love Annie shared or, of which, she was even fully aware. She was flattered by the younger boy's constant attention but never attributed it to anything more than friendship. When she became engaged to Samuel Shell, the son of a local banker, she had no idea of the event's affect on young Bill White. She didn't even notice the sudden cessation of his visits to the local Sonic Drive-in where she had worked for a period of time after graduating from high school.

Yet, Bill was enraged. Other kids his age had often told him he was crazy if he thought he had a chance with her. He had even rationalized that he would first have to get through high school before his chances would improve, but he was furious that she had made the decision to get engaged without talking to him first. She had no right.

For weeks Bill vented his fury relentlessly on a variety of targets. He would beat his mother, younger kids that he found outside alone, and drove out of town shooting at cattle, dogs, or anything he could find. Fortunately most kids already knew to avoid Bill like the plague and his aim with his twenty two caliber pistol was so poor he rarely hit an animal. It was his poor mother, whose husband had long since abandoned them, who suffered the brunt of Bill's ravings.

Bill might have ultimately snapped at that point of his life if it wasn't for the law stepping in. On one of his countryside shooting sprees, a local rancher spotted Bill shooting at his livestock. The rancher gathered up some of his ranch hands, armed themselves, and took off after Bill with the thought of some old western justice of their own. They caught up with Bill about three miles south of Denton, disarmed him, and proceeded to teach him the errors of his ways. Luckily for Bill, another car came by with two teachers from the local high school. They were able to stop the beating and convince the ranchers to turn the matter over to the police. Although Bill's life was never in real danger from the ranch hands, the whipping they had given him made its point. That, combined with a year's probation under what seemed like constant observation by a juvenile probation officer, and Bill's slide into total insanity and a life of crime was temporarily delayed.

Over the next three years Bill lived a fairly normal life. He was certainly no angel, but even his mother had begun to hope that her son might have a future other than violence and crime like his father. Bill graduated from high school close to the bottom of his class, but he graduated. That fact alone was a source of pride for both Bill and his mother. College was not an option for Bill. His grades were poor, his family had virtually no money and he had no appreciation for college aid programs. Besides, Bill had already decided he wanted to be a Marine. He was fascinated with war movies and with the violence and killings he witnessed on the screen.

Shortly after graduation, Bill contacted the local recruiter and signed up. He had to take some physical tests and do some other paperwork but it wasn't long before he was told that he was accepted into the Marine Corps. They didn't have a slot for him until the first of the year so Bill found a temporary job with a road crew that was paving a stretch of road on the outskirts of Denton.

Unfortunately for Annie Shell, it was the same stretch of road she used when she occasionally visited her grandmother. Bill had never totally put her out of his mind, but he had not thought of her much in the past couple of years, primarily because he simply never saw her.

Shortly after starting work with the road team, Bill noticed her drive by. He had the easy job of holding up the "Slow" sign to cars as they went past. The first time she passed she didn't recognize him and he didn't try to get her attention. He was too struck with how beautiful she had become. He waited all afternoon for her to drive back by but she never came. He lingered as long as he could after the team shut down for the day but finally had to leave as the sun began to set.

From that day on he was a model employee. He never missed a day of work, arrived early and stayed late. He never complained. His motivation, however, was not the job but rather the desire to see Annie again. It was nearly a week before she came by again. This time he shouted at her and when she stopped he went up to the car and said hello. She was genuinely pleased to see Bill and expressed amazement on his becoming a man. They only talked for a minute or two as another car came up behind her and she had to move on, but the hook had been reset. Bill was once more obsessed with her.

Over the next three months Bill waved and chatted with

Annie on several occasions. They never saw each other anywhere else. In Bill's own warped mind though he could not envision a life without her and began to convince himself that if given a choice she would certainly run off with him. He had to leave on the seventh of January for Marine boot camp training in San Diego.

He spent all of December planning how to make his move. Twice he purchased a Christmas card for Annie and twice he threw it away. He was torn between his desire to send her a card and the need to keep his plans and his association with Annie a complete secret. He knew Annie expected a Christmas card from him, but in the end, Bill sent no card. The card would have not made any difference as Annie had no idea of the extent of his feelings. Besides she received dozens of cards from old friends in town. Neither she nor her husband would have given the card a second thought.

Bill had selected Monday, the fifth of January as the day to make his move since that would be the first day everyone would be back at work after the holidays. He also knew he needed to give Annie enough time to get organized and packed for the trip to California. He wanted to be able to approach her while Sam was out of the house. It would be best if Sam never knew what happened until after she was gone. Undoubtedly Sam would be mad and hurt at Annie's departure, but that would be his problem.

Bill arrived at the house at ten in the morning. Annie was surprised to see him but immediately let him in and offered him a cup of coffee.

She told him she was babysitting a neighbor's grandson.

The baby was sleeping on a small cot in the living room. They moved to the kitchen. Once there she sat down at the small table pushed against the sliding glass door that went out into the back yard. For a few minutes they talked about the holidays. Realizing that Bill had something on his mind but was reluctant to get to the point, she stood up and opened the sliding glass door and pointed out the new fence she and Sam were putting up. Bill looked out the open door and saw a cement fence about five feet high that was already about halfway complete behind the house.

Something began to snap in Bill's mind. He began to realize that in almost every sentence Annie was talking about herself and Sam. It wasn't right. She had to put Sam behind her. He told her that he had joined the Marines and would be leaving for California in two days. He told her that this was their opportunity to get away from Denton and live together in California, maybe even get married and have children of their own.

The reaction he got was not one he had ever imagined. She looked at him and asked him incredulously if he was crazy. It was only after asking him this that the concept that yes, Bill could be crazy, arrived at full speed into Annie's mind. She backed up and told Bill to leave.

Bill started to argue, expressing his love for her. He had already made up his mind that he was not leaving without her. He was between her and the two exits out of the kitchen, the open door to the back yard and the hall back to the living room and the front door. She tried to talk to him logically, but he grabbed her and tried to kiss her. She struggled, somehow breaking free, and screamed she would call the police.

The mention of the police infuriated him. Why had she been leading him on all these years, just to now threaten him with the police? He lunged at her as she ran out of the kitchen toward the front door, knocking her across the room and into the ironing board. She fell in a tangle with the ironing board and iron. Bill was on top of her in an instant. Annie began kicking and hitting at him with the frenzy of a person fighting for her survival. She kicked Bill hard in the stomach and slapped firmly across his face but Annie's struggle was fruitless. Bill picked the iron up from the floor and began repeatedly striking her head with it. She was dead long before he stopped hitting her.

He smiled as he looked down at her. In his own warped mind, he thought that perhaps now Annie finally realized that she was his. He leaned over and kissed her broken head and sniffed deeply to smell her blood. He wanted to pick her up and hug her and take her with him, but he knew he couldn't. Bill instinctively knew he should move and get out of the house but he was overcome with a feeling of euphoria and of power. He stood there and looked down at her and smiled. It was at that moment that he first realized the thrill that killing would bring to him many more times in his life.

To remove his fingerprints from the iron, he rubbed her skirt repeatedly over the entire iron. He was sure he had not touched anything else. After one last glance at the dead body of Annie Shell, Bill left the house, using his shirt tail to avoid leaving any fingerprints on the door knob. Once outside he walked casually to the end of the block where he had parked his car.

Fate played two tricks that day. Both ultimately cost lives, but one did spare a life for almost two decades. The first, unfortunately, cost a lonely drifter and petty thief his life. Ultimately blamed for the murder of Annie Shell, his only involvement was cutting through a residential alley just to see an open sliding glass door on the back of a house. Just inside the open door, he could see a purse sitting on top of a small table. It just took a few seconds to get to the purse, open it, snatch the wallet and be gone. He never knew there was a dead body in the house.

The second twist of fate led Bill to leave the house without turning around and looking back at a small boy. Luke Fenster, who was just two years old that day, was propped up a little on one elbow after having been awakened by the struggle at the other end of the room. While his eyes were wide open, he fortunately was still in a daze from his sleep and remained silent until after Bill left the house. He then got up and went to Annie. He knew something was wrong and instinctively tried to get out the front door to find his grandmother. As he couldn't quite reach and work the doorknob, he went back and cuddled up next to Annie Shell and finally fell back to sleep.

It was two days later before Bill even remembered that he had left a "witness" behind. But even then he believed the child was still asleep. Besides, he had seen in the papers that the police had just taken credit for discovering who the killer was. Some drifter had been blamed. Bill smiled to himself as he boarded the bus to take him to California.

Chapter 9

Bill's stint with the military did not last very long. In fact, he barely made it through boot camp. Not that he wasn't in good enough physical shape, it was just that his attitude was too warped to be molded by the Corps. Shortly after his first assignment to Camp Lajeune, North Carolina, in a fit of anger for being ridiculed, Bill hit a sergeant with a bucket of paint. After a brief period in confinement, he was discharged from the military. Specifically, he was characterized as unsuitable for continued military service. Bill did not try to appeal the discharge.

After leaving the military, Bill remained in North Carolina and worked for a small fishing outfit on the Atlantic coast that fished out in Onslow Bay. Bill wasn't enamored with North Carolina, but he wasn't going to leave the state until he could exact his revenge on the sergeant who had pressed charges against him. The job kept him close to the large Marine camp.

Nearly a year after his discharge, Bill made his move. He knew that the sergeant was an avid fisherman, often leaving early Saturday morning with friends or alone to one of the nearby lakes to spend the day. Bill had already followed him on a couple of Saturdays waiting for him to be alone. On his third attempt, his target finally left on his own and did not stop to pick anyone up on his way. Bill followed the sergeant, remaining far behind, as he could tell which lake was the final destination from the route he would take out of town. Once at the lake, he watched the sergeant put his small boat in the water and set off for some deserted corner where he could fish without competition.

Bill had intended to walk around to an appropriate spot in order to get close to his target.   He was immediately discouraged, however, when he saw the size of the lake. Unfortunately for the sergeant, the small marina rented fishing boats. Using almost every cent he had with him Bill was able to rent a boat for half a day. The expense discouraged him a little but he kept reminding himself of the prize at the end of the chase.

Following someone on an open lake was not difficult, but when his prey turned the bend and got in close to the shore in one of the lake's many small inlets, Bill thought he had lost him. It was only a matter of time though, as he finally spotted his prey fishing about twenty feet from shore in a narrow inlet surrounded by thick shrubs and tall pine trees. No one else could be seen from this well secluded spot. Perfect, thought Bill, as he steered his boat steadily at his target.

Bill pulled the visor of his baseball cap lower and looked down to hide most of his face. As he pulled in within yards of the other boat he shifted the engine to idle. The sergeant mumbled, "Can't you find your own spot?" Then as Bill lifted his face, recognition then fear set in the sergeant's face. Bill simply smiled, raised his .9mm Beretta and fired once, almost point blank at his victim's head. The sergeant immediately fell backwards into the water. One thing he did learn from the Marines, Bill thought with a grin, was how to shoot. The one shot had entered through the left eye and had killed the man immediately.

Bill took the boat directly back to the marina. He passed no one on the lake and didn't think the shot had caught anyone's attention. Out here in the country an occasional gun shot would cause little concern. He tied the boat to the same slot at the pier where it was when he rented it, and left without speaking to anyone. Fortunately the staff at the marina had their attention directed towards other customers and did not give his departure a second thought. If anyone had heard the gun shot, he couldn't tell.

A month later to the day, Bill was startled when he was confronted by two plain clothed police detectives as he left his small apartment. They wanted to talk to him about the death of a Marine sergeant at a nearby lake. They told him that they had reason to believe someone that looked a lot like him had rented a boat at the lake the same day the sergeant was murdered. Bill's first instinct was to deny being there. When they persisted he told them he was going to complain about their harassing him to his congressman and the mayor. His belligerent attitude was enough to dissuade the detectives. He realized at the same time, though, that by angering them they would only continue to dig deeper. Undoubtedly the detectives were acting on more than just his looks, no matter what they had told him. He knew he had to act fast and an idea that had already been simmering on the edges of his mind became his perfect escape plan.

The owner of the Sea Prince, the boat he was usually assigned to by the small fishing company that employed him, was an individual Bill had quickly begun to loath. Just like many of the sergeants he had dealt with in the Marines, Captain Jones was dogmatic and had no patience with Bill. Feeding him to the sharks was something Bill thought would be a pleasure. In fact, Bill had often gone over in his own mind how he could do it. Usually just three fisherman, counting Jones, would go out on the boat. The longer outings could last twenty four hours, although usually they were back in before that. The Sea Prince was an older fishing boat but had been retrofitted with some of the more modern electronics and navigation equipment found on newer models. The upgrades allowed the Sea Prince to be out at night with little threat of either getting lost or being hit by another ship.

Just two days after being interviewed by the detectives, Bill, Captain Jones and Manuel "Manny" Johnson motored from the pier, and departed through the narrow channel out into the open sea. The sun had not yet risen, but from the brightening sky in the east, it looked like the day would be another pleasant one. For the last week the region's weather had been dominated by two high pressure systems that had kept the skies clear and the seas calm. There had been forecasts of a front moving in but it was still at least a day out.

Bill was pleased that day that there were only the three of them on the boat. It would make things easier. Manny was not a bad guy. Bill even liked him. But he was a perfect candidate for the role Bill had planned out for his own future. Manny was Puerto Rican by birth, but was adopted at a young age by Beth and Frank Johnson, of Orlando, Florida. He never knew who his birth parents were and never really cared to know. His adopted parents had been good to him but at the age of seventeen he had left home and had not kept in touch. In conversations with Bill, Manny had said that it had been nearly seven years since he had any contact with his adopted parents. Manny was still single and lived alone in an apartment not far from the beach. Nobody would miss Manny and nobody would look for him.

Captain Jones took the boat out ten miles before they started fishing. Many of the stretches along the coast had been over fished and the fishing trade was not like it had been, but there were still numerous businesses and restaurants that kept the demand for fresh local fish going. Bill wasn't an avid fisherman but he liked the solitude of the sea and he enjoyed killing the larger fish brought on board. The larger the fish the greater the thrill Bill got from slicing it open.

Bill spent most of the day just mechanically going through the motions of his job. Neither his mind nor his interest were in the work he was performing. He was biding time until the sun turned fiery red and sank into the sea to the west. Bill was usually fascinated with the illusion of the sun sinking into the ocean, but today it was simply his signal to set his plan into motion.

Manny had been talking to Captain Jones about the day's catch and trying to convince the Captain to return to the harbor. When Manny left to use the small rest room on board the boat, Bill made his move.

As the captain stood at the wheel of the ship looking forward, Bill simply walked up behind him and smashed in the back of his head with the baseball bat the crew kept on board. Captain Jones never knew what hit him. As he collapsed, Bill struck him two more times. Moving quickly, Bill dragged him to the rear of the boat, poured a small bucket of "chum" down the back of the captains t-shirt and threw him over board. Bill smiled. The chum was for good luck. Within an hour or two, Captain Jones would indeed be shark food.

Bill had moved quickly to dispose of Captain Jones, but he had not needed to. Manny did not emerge from below for another five minutes. Bill had positioned himself in the stern of the boat crouched down as though he was working intently over some tangled line. He heard Manny approach him but acted as though he was lost in concentration over the tangled line. Manny spoke to him and Bill looked back at him. Manny asked where the captain was and Bill pointed to the front of the boat. As Manny turned around to take a better look, Bill stood up and with the same bat proceeded to strike Manny in the same way he did the captain.

In his perverse mind, Bill decided to treat Manny's ultimate demise with more respect than that of Captain Jones. So he did not place any chum inside Manny's shirt, he simply tied the heavy tool chest to a fishing line that he strapped around Manny's wrist. After he let the boat put a little more distance between them and the point where he threw the captain's body overboard, he dumped Manny's over as well.

At this point he turned the ship back to the west. He wanted to be able to see the shore lights before he made his next move. The winds had picked up and clouds were finally moving in but the weather was still holding for Bill's plan. While enroute back towards the coast, Bill broke into the small lockers that the crewmen and captain used to store their valuables while on board. He found nearly two hundred dollars in the captain's locker and another thirty in Manny's. He already had every penny that he owned with him. More importantly he took Manny's driver's license, a few other cards that could be used for identification, and Manny's apartment keys. When the lights from shore began to penetrate the darkness, he put the engine in idle and went back to the rear of the boat. The Sea Prince had a small aluminum life boat as did most small fishing boats, but it also had an inflatable one that the captain had purchased in the past month. Bill was hoping not many people would remember it. He inflated it with the small air pump on board, connected its small engine to it, and threw it overboard. After tying it to the boat with the safety line he had held onto, he returned to the controls of the Sea Prince. He steered the boat to a southeasterly direction and locked its rudder and speed controls. He didn't want the boat to be going too fast and draw attention, but at the same time he needed it to maintain course and go as far as possible before it was discovered.

Once he felt everything was set, he untied the small lifeboat and leapt to it. He landed short but quickly pulled himself on board. He sat and watched the Sea Prince move steadily away. There wasn't another boat in sight. As he started the engine and turned the lifeboat in the direction of shore, Bill momentarily panicked as he realized he was too low to see the lights that marked the shoreline still miles to the west. But he thought he knew which way it was and he confirmed his intuition by looking back at the fading Sea Prince, which was definitely moving away from shore.

In just a few minutes the lights from the shore reappeared.

Bill steered towards them but was careful not to get too close to any concentration of lights. He was not sure where he was but he did not want anyone to see him arrive on the beach. He took the small craft further south along the coast where the lights began to disappear. Finally feeling safe he took it onto the beach. Once on sand, Bill jumped out, unattached the engine and dropped it back out into about four feet of water. He filled the small fuel tank with water and threw it out even deeper. He then dragged the small inflatable inland to an area of dense underbrush and a small inland pool. He simply left the life boat there concealed by the shrubbery.

The next step he knew would be the most difficult. Bill needed to find his way back to Manny's apartment before anyone started missing them. He walked back to the beach and followed it back to the lights he had seen from the sea. The thirty minute hike into the soft breeze helped dry out his shorts and t-shirt. As he approached the lights he realized that he had come upon a small residential area. The lights to most of the houses were off. He contemplated breaking into one to try to find some car keys but decided to keep pressing on to the denser patch of bright lights.

His luck held as the lights belonged to a Trash Management truck holding area, where it seemed like hundreds of trucks lined the fence. There was some movement in the yard and a few trucks were moving around. He stumbled upon the gate before he meant to and was confronted by a security guard. Surprised, Bill fought the urge to run. He muttered something to the effect he was having problems with his parents and was no longer welcome at home and was looking for a ride back to

Jacksonville. The guard grinned at Bill's alleged predicament and waved down a truck approaching the gate from inside the compound. Within an hour Bill was back in town. He was dropped off only a block or two from Manny's apartment. The sun had not yet made its appearance in the east over the Atlantic and the slow moving, ghostly Sea Prince.

All was quiet at Manny's apartment. There were no police or any other security personnel hanging about. If anyone had raised an alarm about the missing boat it had not yet led to Manny's apartment. Bill let himself in and quickly searched the small two rooms for any valuables or cash he could take. Secondly, and just as important to his plan, he was seeking any documentation he might be able to use later to verify his new identity. He was surprised how little of either that he could find. Other than a laptop computer that he took to pawn later, there was virtually nothing worth taking in the apartment. Furthermore, other than a small address book of dubious value, he found nothing he could use to assist in his identity change. He did take a sweatshirt he could throw over his own t-shirt and a new pair of dry socks.

From the apartment, Bill went straight to the bus station and bought a one way ticket to Washington DC. The bus left just as the sun was rising. Other than to change buses and grab a bite to eat in Raleigh, he slept the entire way. Once in DC, Bill rented the cheapest room he could find in a run down part of town.

Perhaps because of the ride in the Trash Management truck to Jacksonville, Bill hired on with the local trash collection company, as Manny Johnson. It was a simple thing to do. He then began a career in a line of work that he had never considered until his ride the few nights before. A perfect way, he imagined, to stay invisible to society at large.

It was there in the nation's capital where Bill honed his killing skills and truly developed into a full fledged serial killer. Bill took perverse pride in the fact that for the many years that Washington was dubbed the nation's murder capital, he personally deserved some of the credit. Killing was easy in D.C., as the homeless and prostitutes abounded. It took little effort to get one alone. He experimented with drugging his victims and liked the power it gave him over them. It made domination easier and total. He could get them into his apartment without a struggle, then tie and gag them and wait for them to regain their senses. Bill always preferred to kill someone who was fully conscious and aware of what he intended to do to them. Death did not have to come swiftly either. He would often experiment.

Bill purposely targeted the homeless and prostitutes for his victims. Even if they escaped before he got them into his apartment, they virtually never went to the police. In their own warped minds, assaults and danger came with the lifestyle. Besides, they knew few cared.

Only once did he have a brush with the law. He had only been in DC a year and had tried to beat a prostitute to death in his car. She had put up one hell of a fight and had managed to escape. As she ran out of the alley where he had parked with her, she ran in front of a police car that had been cruising the neighborhood. They stopped, assisted her and proceeded to arrest Bill. Bill knew better than to deny striking the prostitute but claimed he did so only in self defense as she tried to rob him. He was taken downtown to be booked for assault.

As luck often held for Bill, it did so again in this case. The policewoman who took his victim to the hospital for a quick check before bringing her to the police precinct made the mistake of not staying with her. At her first opportunity, the prostitute left by a back door and was never seen again by the police.

Without the witness charges were never filed against Bill, but he had learned a lesson. It was shortly thereafter that he began experimenting with doping his victims. He knew the police would not have to dig too far to find out who he really was. He did not want to have to flee the Washington D.C. area as, in his own mind, he had it made there. Not that he was killing people every day, but two or three times a year when the urge needed to be satisfied.

Obtaining the drugs required little effort. A number of his fellow employees used a variety of illegal drugs. Once they became comfortable with Bill as a fellow employee, they readily discussed their abuse and introduced him to their supplier. The whole lack of security seemed incredulous to Bill, but then again, he thought most of his fellow employees were morons. Actually, when it came right down to it, Bill thought most people were idiots or at least significantly inferior to himself.

Getting rid of the bodies of his victims was also not really a problem. His job with the trash collection gave him access to heavy duty trash bags and strong cleaning chemicals. He would simply remove the bodies from his apartment in the large trash bags, often dumping them in trash dumpsters that were on his own route. The residual thrill of watching the truck lift a dumpster, that he knew held one of his victims, up over the truck's cab and then empty its contents in the compactor in the bed of the truck always put him in a good mood.

Over time, however, as a body was discovered in the landfill and one on a trash barge being taken out to sea, the police investigation began to intensify. The news and even the radio talk shows started asking the question "was someone killing the people of the night in D.C.?"

When the police made their second visit to interview the employees of Bill's waste disposal company, Bill realized that it was time to leave. He knew that employees always were quitting without notice and no one seemed to care. Bill had planned long before for a quick get away.

A year and a half earlier, one of his victims had been a homeless man whom he had gotten to know on the streets before he ultimately killed him. The man had been a widower, without children. He had a brother who lived in New York, but with whom he had not corresponded in years. When Bill had killed him, he was somewhat surprised to find a current driver's license and seventy five dollars in the man's wallet. Of the homeless he had killed, few had wallets and none had a current driver's license. More significantly, though, he also found a bank statement that had showed steady four hundred and seventy five dollar monthly deposits since the beginning of the year. There was over twelve thousand dollars in the account. The statement included his victim's social security number and the address to a local Post Office and a box number. Going back over the dead man's clothing, he found a small key that went to the box. He hung onto the driver's license, thinking at the time that it could come in useful if he had to again change his identity and move on. He began to experiment with hair dyes and make-up to find which combination made him look most like the small picture in the license.

He began to pick up the man's mail. There was very little, mostly advertisements. The deposits, which he figured had to be from a pension, continued going straight into the account. He was afraid to correspond with the bank, but his fortunes improved when the bank was bought out by a larger one and he was sent a new signature card and a new ATM card. Bill had never had an ATM card and took full advantage of "his" new one.

Now it was time to leave. Although he was fairly certain that no one would miss him, Bill took the precaution of leaving the city late Friday by bus. He bought a ticket to Los Angeles under his new identity. Prior to leaving, he picked up his paycheck and told the pay clerk to let the management know he wouldn't be back. He made some comment about moving to Florida and left without further elaboration. He doubted that the pay clerk would even pass along the message.

The bus trip was uneventful until he was well into his second full day when he realized that the route was taking him straight through Denton, New Mexico, the lazy western town where he grew up. The bus did not slow down as it zoomed through Bill's hometown. It did not stop until it got to Albuquerque. As it did, though, Bill grabbed his few possessions and jumped off the bus at the station.

In Albuquerque Bill went to a dollar store and got some

makeup and baby powder for his hair. He then booked himself on a bus heading back east with a stop in Denton.

It wasn't a desire to see his mother or any other old acquaintances that drove him to suddenly change his itinerary. He simply had remembered the stories he had heard as a youngster about how one could buy a small parcel of land out in this part of New Mexico for almost nothing and get away from the rest the world. People were pleasant and neighborly but they left you well enough alone, too, if you wanted privacy.

One story that he remembered especially influenced him to turn around and return to Denton. It was of an elderly man, who lived alone on a small ranch not far from town. He lived a hermit like existence, discouraging visitors and only going out when it was necessary. After the local electric company had turned the power off for failure to pay, someone at the utility company finally thought something might be wrong. A deputy sheriff was sent out with a representative from the company. They found the old man dead in his rocking chair. The county coroner estimated that he had been dead for over four months.

Bill chuckled to himself and wondered if anyone had ever bought that old man's small ranch. When his bus arrived at Denton, he jumped out and soon found himself walking by the old Denton High School. He had no special reason to visit the school. He was just drawn to it and it wasn't far from the bus station. School was out for the day but groups of students were on the athletic fields practicing their different sports. He smiled, he was home.

He considered going to see his mother, but walking further past his old house he realized a different family now occupied the house. This angered him a little, primarily towards his mother for moving on rather than waiting for him to return. The fact that he had not corresponded with his mother since he left the Marines over a decade earlier and that she had no way of knowing how to contact him, did not temper his anger towards his mother. She simply should have waited. Bill made no attempt to find out where she may have gone or what may have ever happened to her.

The sun was getting lower and it dawned on Bill that if he had any hopes of finding a used car lot open he better move on. He walked back towards the bus station. He recalled seeing a couple of small car dealers just across the highway from the bus station. Only one was still open for business, but they had what he wanted, a five year old, basic pick-up truck with just enough dents and scratches to make it relatively inexpensive. After contacting the bank Bill was using under his new alias and verifying there was money to cover the five thousand dollar check, the car dealer handed Bill the keys to the pick-up truck. Bill was by no means poor, but he did not plan on having to work again and knew he would have to be careful in how he spent his money. Just in his mid thirties, Bill thought he had already figured out the perfect retirement plan. Steal someone else's.

While at the car dealer, he noticed that one of the salesmen was a high school classmate of his. He walked by the individual and nodded hello. The former classmate grunted something back but gave no indication that he had any idea who Bill was. Bill slept soundly that night in his truck, content in his own mind that things just couldn't get any better. From now on though he knew he would have to better conceal his true identity. In the dim light of the dawn, in his newly purchased pick up, Bill practiced with the wig and make up to perfect his new look.

The next two days Bill industriously set out to find the perfect piece of property. It wasn't that hard to do. A local Realtor finally steered him to a ten acre parcel of land a few miles out of town. The land had a fairly run down but functional house on it. The property bordered a larger ranch. For many years the owner of the larger ranch had paid the owner of the smaller parcel a fee so his cattle could graze on both ranches. Although the payment was not very much it did help subsidize the mortgage payments on the smaller ranch. Furthermore, as the property had been vacant for so long, the realtor was sure that Bill could move right in, renting the property from the bank until the mortgage went through.

By the end of the week Bill was in the old house. He cleaned it sufficiently to meet his needs and had purchased some used furniture at garage sales and at a used furniture store. He had paced off the land and was surprised at how big ten acres felt to him. His associates in Washington D.C. would never have believed that ten acres and a house could be bought so cheaply. Their problem, Bill thought. If they were smart like him, they would have moved out here, too.

As the realtor had mentioned to him, the owner of the adjacent ranch soon got in touch with him and offered to pay him for the use of his land. Bill agreed without haggling. Everything was done by phone. Monthly thereafter a small check arrived by mail to Bill. He never did meet his neighbor.

Bill began subscribing to survivalist magazines and started a small garden that actually did quite well. He avoided people and rarely went to town during the daylight hours. Money-wise he was barely staying even. But life was good and soon he began his hunting. There simply were no homeless in Denton and while he had no doubt that there were prostitutes, they weren't the easy prey that stood openly on the street corners in D.C.. In fact, he never did see one.

It wasn't too hard, though, to find a different kind of prey. Hitchhikers now became his targets, as did the hobo's and kids that illegally rode the freight trains that seemed to trace the route of the old Route Sixty-six or the newer interstate highway through New Mexico from the Midwest to the Pacific coast.

In many ways, the hunt became more exciting for Bill. He never knew when he would find a victim or exactly where. He ran into his first train jumper by accident. Searching for hitchhikers, he picked up a talkative twenty two year old young man who explained to him how jumping onto trains for rides across the country was a 'blast' and how several young people were doing it now. The thrill of the ride and avoiding the law was something that grew on you. He further explained how many people get off in towns like Denton to avoid the security in the larger cities. There was an old railway bridge just four miles east of Denton that caused the trains to slow down to a speed safe enough to jump off or get back on. A number of young 'jumpers' and some of the true hobos used the bridge as their boarding and unboarding point.

Hitchhikers and those who stole free rides on trains were the perfect prey. Their disappearance might result in searches and frantic families but there was never a specific travel itinerary that the police could use to pin point the disappearances. For his part, Bill ensured that the bodies were never located.

Frequently Bill was unsuccessful during these hunts. But he was always prepared. He routinely carried a cooler with a half dozen gatorades or other sports drinks on ice. All the drinks in the cooler were drugged with a fairly significant amount of rohypnol. On two occasions, his victims died from the drug dose itself. More often when they came to, they found themselves bound and chained in a windowless basement room in Bill's house. He had become addicted to breaking his victims' will to resist before ultimately killing them.

Acquiring the rohypnol or other similar drugs was easy. He had to go to Albuquerque to purchase it, but finding the sellers in Albuquerque took little effort. He had been well trained in Washington D.C.

For nearly five years life went along uninterrupted for Bill. No one seemed the least bit interested in him. If the law had looked at Denton for possible leads to the disappearances of his victims he was unaware of it.

The fact was that Denton never did come up on the scope at the FBI which had the task to piece together the disappearances of a growing number of transients along the I-40 corridor. The FBI had identified an individual in Santa Fe who was subsequently convicted of killing a drifter. Even though the suspect had only confessed to the one murder, the assumption was that he may have killed some of the other victims that were thought to have disappeared in New Mexico.

Bill, in his own way, felt like he had set up roots in Denton and was content with his existence. After all this time, he did not want to go on the run again. He just had to tie up this one loose end, Sarah Stone. Then he could keep a low profile for months until the heat went away.

Chapter 10

"So where do you suggest that we begin," Sarah asked, but then continued on, " I think Rick must have had a point when he said that the murderer of poor Annie Shell was not the drifter after all. It would fit with Luke's reaction when remembering his second birthday."

"Well, I agree his reaction was probably caused by his remembering the murder, but that doesn't mean the drifter didn't kill her. Didn't they find Annie's wallet on him?"

"Yes," she replied, "and I know that certainly implicated the drifter, but maybe he just found it along side the road where the other individual, the real murderer, may have dropped it."

"Possibly, but for the sake of a lead, let's suppose you are right. If Luke remembered who the murderer was, that would mean he would have had to have known him. If he did, even at two years old, he could have told the police who it was." I didn't want to admit I really didn't remember if two year olds could even talk yet, but I thought kids started talking earlier.

"I am sure that Luke was talking by then but I don't know how much credibility the police would have given him. Maybe if we talk to the Sheriff, he will fill us in on what all is in the file." Sarah was certainly more optimistic on what she could get out of the Sheriff than I was.

"How about your own newspaper?" I asked.

"I've already looked at that, more than once. There is no

mention of what, if anything, the child may have said. Just that he was uninjured." Sarah continued, as if she could read my mind. "I am sure the Sheriff will talk to us."

We left the restaurant and headed to the Sheriff's office. This time Sarah insisted on paying the bill. I liked this new world.

Our route took us by a small mall where Sarah unexpectedly turned into the parking lot and pulled up close to a Sears. "I suggest you buy a new shirt and maybe some slacks. No offense, but you should know you are looking a little ragged."

I rolled my eyes at her as I got out of the car. She followed me into the store. Once inside, I quickly grabbed a couple of shirts and a pair of khaki slacks and proceeded to the counter. I would come back alone to buy my underwear.

"Whoa!" she instructed, obviously from some rodeo background, "what are you doing? You missed a whole section of the store. There are more shirts and slacks over there. Don't you think we should take a look at those before we rush out?"

"These have places for my arms and legs and are just fine for me. Besides they are on sale." I proceeded to the checkout counter, hoping my comment about being on sale would sway the argument. For whatever reason, she followed me to the register without complaining.

As we got back into the car she got the last word in, "Men are really lousy shoppers," and then for the really nasty cut, "what were you, too embarrassed to buy any underwear with me there?"

I didn't reply, what could I say? I just grinned at her and drove to the Sheriff's office.

Sheriff Gibbs was not in when we arrived. He had driven

over to the State Forensic Lab to discuss the murders with the lab experts. Unless he was delayed, they expected him back shortly after lunch.

As we drove away, I asked Sarah if I could look at the old press coverage of the murder of Annie Shell. If these killings were all connected and that possibility seemed to be increasing, then I needed to get smarter on the initial event. Sarah said there would be no problem in getting to the old records as they were all on microfiche in the archives. Denton hadn't totally gotten into the computer era yet. She explained it was more because of the owners did not see the need to digitize everything than because Denton was behind the times technically. I didn't really care, microfiche was just fine.

The archives were not located with the rest of the Denton newspaper's offices. They occupied a small warehouse just south of the town center. The only employee in the building was a heavyset lady with thinning grey hair whom Sarah introduced to me as Marge, just Marge. Marge proved to be very helpful and friendly. She took us both to the reviewing area, set us both up with coffee, and left us alone with instructions to shout if we needed anything else.

The microfiche was well organized and we found the copies we were looking for in no time at all. Sarah had done this before and had a tendency to rush me though the stories. I had to keep slowing her down. The articles about the incident centered mostly on Annie and her family citing the tragedy and the loss to the community. There was no mention of a break-in. The house was found insecure as the sliding glass door from the kitchen was wide open.

The sheriff should be able to add more. I was looking for something that could explain how the drifter might have stolen the wallet without actually assaulting Annie. The open door certainly could have given him that access.

The news articles acknowledged the baby's presence at the crime scene and mentioned that he was unhurt. They did not elaborate on whether the child had contributed anything to the case. Again, I thought Sheriff Gibbs may be able to answer the questions we had developed.

Marge had come up behind us while we were doing our research and spoke unexpectedly to us. "You all checking up on the old Shell murder?" She could see it on the screen in front of us. "What, may I ask, is your interest in that old killing? That happened almost twenty years ago."

"Do you remember much about it Marge?" I asked.

"Not too much, it happened a couple of years before I started working for the paper. I was a sales clerk at a grocery store back then. A lot of us talked about it. You couldn't blame us. It was the biggest thing that happened to this town in years. But they caught the killer and over time people just stopped talking about it. It was such a tragedy." Suddenly, as though a light went on in her mind, "Hey, wasn't the baby there at the time Luke Fenster, the same Luke who was just murdered?" As I nodded, she continued, "Well slap my face, why didn't I think of that. It's rare enough to be present for one murder, but for two. Unless you are the murderer, I would say the odds are that both killings are related. I don't believe we have had a total of three murders here in town since poor Annie's death. All three of those involved one family member killing another. For these two strange ones to both involve Luke, they have to be related."

While her logic pattern would probably not withstand a defense lawyer's cross examination, she made sense to me and only reinforced our own theory. "Any wild guesses who could have killed Luke and his grandmother, Marge?" asked Sarah.

"No, not at all. Except it has to be someone who lives here. At least a person who lived here then and lives here now. I guess there is no reason to think the person had to live here the whole time in between. But I can't think of anyone in Denton who could have done such a thing. You know I read every line in this paper everyday. I also belong to a bridge club and a bingo group. What I don't learn from the paper, I pick up from the groups. We all love to gossip and I think I know about everyone in town. A lot of it I don't even believe, but even with all I read and hear I would be shocked if someone from Denton is the killer."

"People are often shocked when they find out who a killer is. Some people never accept the fact that their friend or lover is a murderer, even after the individual confesses. But supposing you are correct and no one you know could be the killer, I imagine there is a good fifty per cent of the town you don't know." I wasn't too sure where I was trying to get to, but I wanted to hear a little more of this old west logic.

"Not really, you'd be surprised how much is written in our paper about the kids in school, the church activities, the police blotters, business events, sicknesses and death. Over the years, I have gotten to know about a lot of people. I've learned to follow peoples' lives. Maybe I shouldn't be so nosy, but I guess that's why I like this job. And the ladies in my groups have relations with many other families in this town. We have quite the source net, and as I mentioned, they all love to gossip." She smiled, "I could ask them if they had any theories."

"No, not just yet, Marge. I am not yet sure what we are actually dealing with and I certainly don't want to put anyone else at risk." She looked at Sarah inquisitively. Marge didn't know about my association with Luke and I didn't feel like explaining it.

"Marge, I would like to talk more with you later." I looked at Sarah, "I imagine we both would, but let's break for the day." I just suggested to Sarah that we have a bite to eat for lunch and, after saying our good byes, left the building.

"You cut her off there fairly quick, West. She was just trying to help out." Sarah admonished me.

"I didn't mean to be rude, but I don't want to give our killer any more reason to target anyone else in town. If he thinks we have a lead on him, no matter how shallow, he may again strike at someone. I don't want to do anything that might be dangerous for you, or Marge," I added.

She seemed to accept my point of view. I knew she had become concerned about her own safety. I had already decided to keep a close eye on her the next couple of days. My gut was telling me something was going to break before too long.

"For what it is worth, your friend Marge impressed me. She must be a real asset for the newspaper. The warehouse was well organized and in great shape and she certainly seemed to be on top of what is happening in Denton." I didn't just say this to try to show to Sarah that I thought highly of her friend Marge. I also wanted to reinforce my comment that if I had appeared rude it wasn't because I thought poorly of her friend.

Chapter 11

We grabbed hamburgers at a Sonic drive-in. The atmosphere of the fast food restaurant slowly changed our mood. "This almost feels like our first date," I teasingly commented with a smile.

"If eating at a Sonic is your idea of a date, then I am going to have to start looking for a bigger spender." She responded with a grin of her own. She was easy to talk to, and unlike in my few previous relationships since my divorce, panic didn't seem to be making a move to control my emotions.

I have always known that it wasn't smart to get emotionally involved with someone working the same case or with clients, but in this case I found myself rationalizing away that logic. After all, my male ego had a point, she had to be protected.

"I thought the wait staff at Sonic used to wear roller-skates," I mused. "Maybe that was a different chain."

"This one never has, but you are the second person from whom I have heard that statement. So you may be right. It must have been before my generation." She chuckled to herself.

Her humor about our age difference didn't bother me too much. The fact that it didn't seemed to be a good sign to me. We ate our burgers and fries and talked about different fast food places where we had eaten and tried to think of our favorites. She had never heard of some that I liked.

As we finished I suggested we head over to see if the Sheriff had returned. She agreed and we left the Sonic.

By the time we arrived back at the Sheriff's office, Gibbs had already returned. He was on the phone and we had to wait in the lobby for five or so minutes. When we were able to get in and talk to him, we found him in pretty good spirits.

"The lab verified that the gun that shot Luke and his grandmother was the same used to kill Rick. While I know we all expected that, it is good to get confirmation. We certainly don't want two murderers running around. All individuals were shot at fairly close range. The lab guys think that Rick was left for dead but was somehow able to get into his truck and try to drive back to town." I was pleased that the Sheriff started talking before we had to prompt him.

"Could he have been shot while he was in the car?" I asked.

"Not likely, there was a lot of blood in the car but no real splatter. That bullet took a hunk of flesh out and would have sprayed blood and tissue around the inside of the vehicle. The lab could find no indication of that. They think he was shot outside it and left for dead. He should have been dead, too. But he didn't die right away. When he came to, he staggered back into his Suburban and tried to get to town. He just didn't make it. He must have passed out again. After that, his truck went off the road and ended up where it did. Once more Rick regained consciousness, got out of his car and collapsed where you found him." Gibbs looked at Sarah, "I hope I wasn't too graphic for you, Sarah. I know Rick was a good friend. I liked him too."

"I'm ok," responded Sarah, but it was obvious that she wasn't. "What else did the lab tell you?"

"That's really it. They discounted a number of things, for example, there was no indication of a struggle in any of the killings. In essence, all we really learned was that the bullets came from the same weapon, a nine millimeter, and the ammo was your typical ball ammo you could buy at any store that carries ammunition."

"Any way we could tell if the victims knew the murderer?" I asked.

"There was no sign of a break-in at Luke's, so they likely let the killer in. Don't know if that means they actually knew him. It seems as though Rick sought him out, but I can't tell if he was acquainted with him or just figured something out that is eluding us." The sheriff paused in thought, "I wonder what he figured out that we can't?"

"I don't know," said Sarah, "and it has bothered me. We worked fairly closely together. He was more into sports in the city and state and a little more familiar with things going on outside the city, but that's about it. I discussed his projects last night with the editor and there was nothing either of us could put our fingers on. He must have just had a touch of brilliance that led to his death. I know that sounds crass, but I don't mean for it to." I thought she was going to break down.

"It's only natural to be affected by his death, Sarah. I didn't even know him but I feel bad about it. I also blame myself for getting this terrible stuff started." I confessed.

"Neither one of you should feel the least bit guilty," Gibbs rebutted. "Don't start blaming yourselves for the behavior of some maniac. I do enough of that myself," he ended with a smile. But I thought he was probably telling the truth.

"Sheriff," Sarah wanted to get us back on point, "what can you tell us about the murder of Annie Shell?"

"Well, one thing I can tell you right off the bat, she wasn't shot. She was killed by someone who crushed her skull with an iron. What questions do you have about it? That may be a better way to get to the answers you are seeking."

"Did Luke say anything to describe the killer?" asked Sarah.

"I pulled that file, or what we had left of it, just after you and I talked the other day, West." He opened a desk drawer and pulled out an old file, fairly thin for a murder inquiry. "As you can see, there is not much here. The guys back then were more than happy to close it out quickly and blame that drifter. Guess that made sense at the time. Looking back I wished they had done a little more work. From the crime scene pictures you can see the location of Annie's purse." He passed over a photograph to us. "What do you see?"

"It's on a table," Sarah paused as she studied the picture, "and it's right next to an open sliding glass door, that leads out into the back yard. An easy grab for anyone just walking by."

"Especially if that someone is an experienced thief. The trace on that drifter came back with a number of petty crimes, mostly thefts, but with no indication that he was violent. Plus the other photos show that the fence in the back yard was being worked on and that from the alley anyone walking by could look right in and see the purse. It would have only taken a minute at most to get to the purse, rifle through it, and get back to the alley. The drifter would not have had to even enter the house. But to get back to your question, the only reference to anything Luke may have said was a poorly written reference in one of the deputies inputs that implied to me that Luke just referred to a man hitting Annie. Nothing else."

"That is probably all he did say. If he didn't recognize the guy and it is likely he wouldn't, that's probably all he could contribute. Did they dust for prints?" I asked.

"I believe so, but none were kept after the case was closed. Before digitization, it was common to get rid of documentation that the courts and the police thought were irrelevant. You have to understand that they thought they had their killer. As you know in many murders the spouse is the immediate suspect. They did take a close look at Sam's alibi and it was solid, plus there was no reason other than statistical to think he may have done it." Again the sheriff paused, "In case you are wondering about his location now, he is in San Francisco. I got his phone number from his father and called him this morning. He was there and it would have been very difficult for him to have gotten back so quickly, not impossible, but I can't make the theory work with him as the killer."

"Very thorough, Sheriff, I hadn't thought about him as a suspect." He had obviously already started rolling over all the rocks from the old case. "What is your theory, then, on Annie's murder?"

"I don't really have one. It was most likely a crime of passion. Someone who went there not planning to kill her. For some reason they got into a struggle, maybe the guy made a pass at her and it was rebuffed. I am assuming it was a guy. She rejected it, threatened him and he went crazy. The iron was used as a weapon simply because it was there. If it wasn't the killer would have just grabbed something else."

"Do you think she had a boyfriend?" Sarah again joined the conversation.

"Don't know really, there was absolutely no indication of that at all in the file. But, that certainly doesn't mean there wasn't one. It could have also been someone who was obsessed with her. She may not have even known about the obsession," explained Sheriff Gibbs.

"That means it could be anyone in the whole town," remarked Sarah.

"It is not as daunting a task as you make out, Sarah," I theorized. "Remember, Rick figured it out. At least, he figured it out far enough to get himself killed. Whoever the killer is he can probably be smoked out, but I'm not sure that is the best way to work this. The guy is dangerous and we don't want him to strike out at anyone again. If we could just figure out what Rick did."

"I have his office and his apartment sealed. Two of my deputies went through it to look for anything that might give us a clue and came up empty handed. I kept them both sealed and thought the three of us may want to take a second look. Are you up to it Sarah? If not we could hold off until tomorrow. We need your help, you knew him best, but I can't wait any longer than tomorrow."

"Let's do it today, Sheriff. I'm ok and I would just as soon stay busy. I know how he did his research and how he kept his records. If he has something there I should be able to recognize it."

We all piled in the Sheriff's car and drove to Rick's apartment. I watched Sarah as we entered the apartment. She was handling the situation well. She immediately led us to a filing cabinet in the bedroom that she said he used to file all his work related papers. We attacked the clutter in the cabinet and spent over an hour segregating what was obviously not related to our investigation, such as what looked like historical notes on past rodeos, sports activities and business events. What was left was a short stack of papers that were hard to identify with a specific project. Several papers had nothing more on them than a name, a phone number and a few cryptic words that meant something to Rick but not much to us.

"A couple of these I think I recognize." Sarah stated.

"For example, this one here that says Jim Rogers, has a number and refers to the Red Zebra, I believe is related to a story he wrote a few years ago about a club east of here by the Texas border. It was quite an expose. I believe he described the place as a drug ridden flop-house. For a while he was being sued and then the state moved in and shut the place down. He was nominated for a state wide press award but didn't make the finals. I can only imagine Rogers was a contact he had for part of the story. This other one, I think has to do with a story he did a while back about fishing here in New Mexico. I can probably screen out a couple more if I study them long enough," Sarah offered.

"We'll take these back to the station and copy them. I'll keep the originals and give you a copy, Sarah, to do whatever magic you can with them. West, you want a copy? You can have one too," Sheriff Gibbs offered. "Let's move on to the rest of the apartment."

We spent another hour looking for anything of relevance

and found nothing. We then moved to Rick's office at the newspaper. We were joined by the paper's senior editor, Tony Swit, at the office. He offered to help but kept his distance. Swit was a big jovial looking guy. I thought at Christmas he probably was frequently asked to play Santa. We grabbed a few extraneous notes that we couldn't immediately discount, but that was all. Neither search seemed to bear much promise. The Sheriff took advantage of Swit's offer and made copies of all the documents seized from both searches and gave copies to Sarah.

As Gibbs drove us back to his offices, there was a distinct air of depression that radiated from us all. I'm not sure if it was a result of not finding something significant or simply because we were all slowly becoming stressed.

"I'm sorry, I wasn't more help," mentioned Sarah.

"Don't get negative on us yet," I told her. "You may be able to piece something together from the copies you have. Also, I've been thinking, did Rick have any drinking buddies or other pals that he may have confided in?"

"A couple but let me think about it. I should be able to come up with a list by tomorrow." She was obviously tired.

We went into the Sheriff's office for about fifteen minutes to work out a short range plan. Sarah was assigned the task of studying the seized papers and to write up a list of Rick's friends. Sheriff Gibbs was going to query the FBI and the State police to see if they had any ideas or could match any of the evidence to anything they were working. He asked me to come up with whatever theories I could that we could then try to work through. I already had one that I wanted to refine before sharing it. It was something that Marge had mentioned.

"How about dinner somewhere?" I suggested to Sarah after we parted company from Sheriff Gibbs.

"Sure." I was pleased that she said yes. She was looking a little ragged and depressed. I wanted to do what I could to get her out of her funk.

"Do you have a favorite restaurant here in Denton?" I asked.

She named a small spaghetti house not far from the high school.

We went there and stayed until they closed the place. The restaurant wasn't crowded.   After we finished eating what surprised me as a very good meal, we stayed and talked over coffee and wine for a couple of hours. The time went by fast. Sarah was in a talkative mood and I let her ramble on. It could only do her good. Plus I was interested in learning more about her. She had most certainly gotten under my skin.

"I guess you could say I grew up in what might be referred to as a typical middle class, American family. I participated in girl scouts and a number of other school activities. I loved riding horses and participating in local events. When I was fifteen, I came in second place in the local rodeo queen competition held in conjunction with the county fair."

"I'm impressed." I responded, and in truth I was.

As the conversation continued I learned that she was a horseback barrel racer and loved to snow ski. The latter she perfected while attending New Mexico State University in Las Cruces, New Mexico. She had been engaged once, while in college, but that fell through when she found her fiancé was a regular visitor to a Mexican brothel in Juarez. She knew a lot of the guys would go down there on weekends, but it was hard for her to accept it. She also thought that it would be hard for her fiancé to break his habits after they were married. It was a thought she couldn't get out of her mind and ultimately led to their break up.

"After I graduated, with a degree in journalism, I returned to Denton and was immediately hired by the local paper."

"Very good."

"It wasn't very difficult. As you can imagine there is no abundance of journalists looking to come to Denton to find work." Sarah remarked. Even Rick had been local.

Her life after college primarily revolved around her job, which she loved. She thought she was a good reporter. I imagined she was. Denton was an easy town to work in. The paper was accepted as part of the town. Most of the population subscribed to it and the paper, on its part, supported the town. Her comments prompted a question whether any of the local kooks had ever threatened the paper or Rick.

"No" she responded. "A few people would disagree with something the paper said, but the paper has a policy to always print those comments so the rest of the community could see an alternative view. I think the practice works really well and kept animosity to a minimum."

Besides, she went on, Denton was a peaceful town. In many ways it was like a big family. It had its squabbles but overall everyone got along. The whole town turned out for the county fair and for the high school football games. When a fire burned down two homes on the west side a few years ago, most of the town helped the families rebuild.

She had recently bought a house and other than getting married and having some children of her own, thought she had pretty well achieved success. She was not rich but had enough money to buy what she wanted and stay relatively debt free.

Rick's murder had really turned her world upside down. She was quite fond of Rick and many in town had expected the two of them to get married. It wasn't going to happen, Sarah said. They were good friends. They had tried dating, simply for the same reason others thought they were a perfect match. They were both single, about the same age, and worked together. But there was simply no magic and over time there was no real desire by either to date each other. Ultimately they stopped dating. They remained friends and would still frequently have lunch together during work but that was it.

I wasn't totally convinced there hadn't been more to it, but there was no use pressing the issue. It would have also been in bad taste. Whatever their deeper relationship had been, it had abruptly come to an end.

Finally we realized they had closed up the restaurant around us. The management was polite enough not to rush us but we got the hint and finally departed.

We had been in her car and from the restaurant she drove to my hotel. I was going to just jump out and thank her for chauffeuring me around all day but she pulled in and parked. She got out of the car when I did. She gave me a funny look and said, "Don't worry Romeo this is not going to be your lucky night." I chuckled and she continued, "I would prefer to work out the list of Rick's friends tonight and not dwell on it. If you don't mind, Jim, it should just take a few minutes."

"That's fine with me, I don't mind at all. Would you prefer to work on the list in the lobby or up in my room?"

"I imagine the room would be quieter and much more private."

Once in the room we discussed what our objective was for the list. I explained to her that we needed the names of any individuals that she thought Rick was close enough to discuss his work with or to bounce theories off. It could be a golfing buddy, a drinking buddy or a mentor. We discussed a few names and as she described Rick's relationship with them, I told her to put their names on the list. When she finally pulled out a piece of hotel stationary to start the list, I told her I was going to lie down on the bed and just rest my eyes. It had been a long day and I still had to piece together my theory on what had happened to cause the killings.

All of a sudden I realized I had been asleep and awoke with a start. I sat up and noticed only the small lamp at the desk was still on. The overhead light had been turned off and I assumed Sarah had left rather than waking me up. Then I saw her on the sofa across the small room. She was stretched out with the extra blanket from the closet covering her. She was asleep. I got up and started to go to wake her, but she seemed to be sleeping so peacefully. I thought that this was probably the same dilemma she faced an hour or so earlier finding me asleep in my bed. I finally decided the logic she likely used on me was also good for her. Let her sleep. I adjusted the blanket over her, went and turned off the lamp at the desk, and returned to the bed. I lay there and looked at her for a while until I finally dozed off.

Chapter 12

Across town, another person was having trouble staying awake, too. Bill White had been waiting patiently for Sarah to come home. He had not thought this was going to be difficult, but if she never showed up he was just wasting his time. Although I didn't know it, about the time I was again falling to sleep for the second time, Bill started up his old pickup truck and drove home. He would try again tomorrow night.

Bill was antsy when he awoke the next morning. He knew there could be a number of reasons Sarah would stay out at night. She may have even left town. As there had been no indication that the police were interested in him he didn't believe she had passed anything on to them. Possibly, Rick didn't tell her anything. More than likely she just didn't put it together yet and Bill was not going to wait for that to happen.

Rick had not really put it all together, but he had gotten it close enough to be killed. Rick had been looking for anyone that had moved back into the Denton area in the past three to five years. In a town the size of Denton that was only a handful of people. Someone had mentioned to Rick that a younger guy had been visiting the old man residing at the home Bill had purchased. No one actually had been visiting, but obviously someone had seen Bill leave the house in his car or working around the small ranch itself without his disguise. Bill had gotten lazy and, at times, did not wear his disguise when he was out and about. Someone must have mentioned it to Rick. Among the other ranchers Rick had questioned that day he had stopped Bill, who was in disguise, to ask him about this younger visitor.

Rick had waved at Bill from his own truck as they both coincidently stopped at an intersection not far from Bill's home. Bill had been returning from town and confused by this stranger waving at him at the intersection, just waved back and drove on. Rick made a u-turn and followed Bill flashing his lights. Bill stopped and Rick got out of the truck and walked up to the side of Bill's pick-up.

During their brief discussion, something in Rick's eyes gave Bill the indication that Rick had either suddenly realized he was wearing a disguise or that he was evading the questions. Whatever it was, Bill White decided to end the interview on the spot. He did so by suddenly pulling out his gun and shooting Rick Jemenez at point blank range in the head. Rick collapsed at the side of the road. After quickly looking around and seeing no one in any direction, Bill floored the accelerator to his pick-up and drove off. He was sure that Rick was dead and was amazed when he heard on the radio where the body was found.

Now, from inside his house looking out, Bill saw the ominous clouds that filled the sky. It looked as though it would be another stormy day. This part of the southwest didn't get a lot of rain, but when it did rain, it often came in the form of violent thunderstorms. Bill thought about going back to Sarah's house and waiting but he knew it would be safer to wait for dark. The rain might give him some cover but it would still be risky. In his frustration he decided to get into his pickup and just drive. He didn't bother with his wig and makeup. He wasn't planning on stopping anywhere.

The wind had picked up but the rain hadn't started. It wouldn't be far behind. The country was wide open in this part of the state and the clouds would whip by close to the ground. As Bill got to the end of his long driveway and started to enter the roadway, a pick up truck with two young men shot by at nearly sixty miles per hour. Bill had to hit his brakes hard not to collide with them. The shock of the close call sent Bill's heart racing. He had been coming out of his driveway for years and he rarely even saw another car on this lonely stretch of road. He had developed a bad habit of hardly slowing down. He didn't know the two young men but had seen them before on his road. They often did jobs of various sorts for a number of the ranchers in the area. After regaining his composure, Bill took his truck out onto the road and headed east.

Dave Hepp and Saul Church cursed at the pick up truck as they shot past it. "That idiot tried to get us all killed." Dave half shouted after they were clear.

Saul concurred and commented, "It's that younger guy again? I tell you Dave that is the third time we've seen him in that old man's truck in the last year or two. I bet they are both queer as can be."

Dave chuckled, "Yep, he probably comes here a couple of times a year just so the two of them can have some hot passionate love." They both laughed at Dave's remark and soon moved on to other topics of conversation.

Bill was driving aimlessly for a half hour when the rain started. A steady wind driven rain kept visibility to a minimum. He thought about heading home when a momentary break in the rain disclosed a train in the distance heading towards Denton. Instinctively he took the next paved road that would cross over to the access road that paralleled the highway.

He had no trouble catching up with the train as it slowed down for the section of the track that went over the old bridge. He passed the train and parked under the cover of an abandoned gas station and country store. These abandoned stations litter the back roads of the west. Before the interstate system they provided a necessary and active convenience. This one was on a section of Route 66 that was now a mile north of I-40. That one mile took all the traffic and it wasn't long after the completion of the interstate that the station had to shut down.

The abandoned gas station was close to the spot where the train jumpers would take advantage of the slowing train to jump clear. It was also on the way to Denton. Anyone sneaking off the train at the bridge would likely walk right by it. Bill sat back and waited. If it had been clear he would have gone down closer to watch but in the rain he figured anyone walking up the road would have to have come from the train. The train passed by and it wasn't another five minutes before two people came running and laughing to the shelter of the old station. As Bill saw them coming he got out of his car, walked around to the front of it and popped open the hood. He leaned in as though he was looking at the engine.

The couple turned out to be a young woman and man. After they tried to lean against the old store front to get out of the rain and had meager success, they both sprinted to the cover of the awning over the gas station pumps.

Bill looked up and feigned surprise. He smiled at the couple and said hello. They ignored him at first but realizing that they were somewhat trapped by the rain decided to be sociable and began talking to Bill. The three talked about the weather and Bill answered their questions about Denton. The two were from Florida and were trying to get to California. They did not elaborate. Bill explained that he thought some water must have gotten into his engine as the truck stalled on him twice. He had pulled into the shelter of the station to check it.

He said he would be happy to give them a ride into the city and they accepted. Bill's adrenalin started surging. He had often thought that what he was feeling at times like this was akin to what the big game hunters felt when their prey first walked into sight. At other times, he compared his emotions to how a lion must feel when it started stalking its prey. Bill never, even for a moment, considered his intense feelings at a moment like this to be the pure insanity of a sadistic mad man.

He wanted this female. Something about her eyes bewitched him, they almost scared him. He wanted to break her. It would be risky to go after them both, but he couldn't resist. He offered them both a Gatorade as he opened the cooler he kept in the back of his truck. He took one for himself that he knew had not been spiked, opened it and took a big swig. Both the male and the female said sure. Bill reached in, took out one at a time, acted as though he was breaking the seal for them and handed each a drink that was drugged with enough rohypnol to knock out a horse. They both took big gulps commenting that they had not had anything to eat or drink in the three hour train ride from Amarillo.

Bill suggested they sit inside his pick up while he finished checking the engine and closing up the hood. They snuggled closely inside. He saw them both take another drink. He didn't care if the guy died from the drug but he wanted her to stay alive.

He got into the cab of the pick up and started the engine. He told the couple he would have to take a short detour as the road ahead had a gully that routinely flooded in this kind of rain. The detour would only add a minute or two to the trip. He turned back the way he had come and headed for his house. The two took another smaller sip. The girl, who was already tired, snuggled up on her friend's shoulder and dozed off. The guy looked at Bill and smiled. Bill held up his Gatorade and offered a toast to the couple's trip. The young man raised his bottle for the toast and took another drink. Bill smiled again. Maybe he could have fun with both. It had been a long time since he had two people to play with. The guy mumbled something about their lucky day catching a ride to stay out of the rain. When he looked over, the guy had his head resting on the girls head. He too had fallen to sleep. Bill smiled and slowly pulled into his long winding driveway. The rain and clouds had become more ominous.

Chapter 13

Sheriff Gibbs looked across the table at Mrs. Gwendolyn Sattler. She was typical of the elderly in Denton. She dressed casually but neat. She carried herself with confidence. Most importantly, she was secure in herself and in Denton, the people in which she now considered her extended family. After living in Denton for just over seventy years, Gwendolyn Sattler personally knew virtually everyone in town. She had a number of close friends her own age. She had seen their children grow up and had attended hundreds of weddings of her friends' children, nieces and nephews. She had seen hundreds of pictures of grandchildren and had listened to more than a thousand stories about how this grandson or that granddaughter had gotten engaged, was picked as class president, or suffered some tragedy. Gwendolyn Sattler was among the age group that volunteered at the church and the hospital, worked at the county fairs and routinely gave unsolicited advice to the city counsel and the business leaders. More often than not the advice was heeded.

Gibbs had known Mrs. Sattler ever since he began work at the Sheriff's department. She was a nice, soft spoken woman. She was not prone to exaggeration or fantasy as some were. He was anxious to hear what she had to say. He had been briefed by one of his staff on what she had to say, but wanted to hear it from her personally.

"Mrs. Sattler, I appreciate your coming here this morning. Hopefully, we'll get you out of here before the rain hits. I know you have been through this before, but if you don't mind would you please tell me about your conversation with Mrs. Fenster."

"I don't mind, Sheriff. It really wasn't much of a conversation but I did notice some concern in Kitty's voice when she mentioned Billy White's name. She said that she thought he was back in town and asked me if I remembered him. I told her that I faintly recalled him. I knew his poor mother a little better. She sure had a rough life. You know, she up and left Denton not long after Billy joined the Marines."

Gibbs knew Kitty was the nickname for Luke's grandmother but he didn't know who Billy White was. The office had already done a trace on the name and had come up with an individual who had died in a boating accident over a decade earlier. "Do you know if she saw this Billy White or why she believed he was in town?"

Gwendolyn answered right away. "Oh, she said she had seen him around. Something about not recognizing him at first. He looked older or something, which I told her - 'don't we all?' I have to admit that I wasn't listening that well. We were all having tea, some of the girls were having coffee, and everyone was talking. I tried not to be rude to Kitty because I could tell she was a little agitated, but Jill Ingram was sitting across from me and she was telling everyone how her granddaughter had caught her husband, a real jerk, in the sack with someone else. I am afraid that story was getting more of my attention. I did ask Kitty who Billy was as I couldn't remember him. She reminded me of his mother and we talked a bit about her. Then I had to leave.   Some of us volunteer at the hospital on Saturday afternoons. I am surprised though if Luke was back here that she didn't mention it. She knows he was always one of my favorites. Sheriff, I sure hope you catch the killer. Luke and Kitty were such nice people."

Sheriff Gibbs and Mrs. Sattler talked a little longer before she departed. He was troubled with the conversation. Finally they had a great lead, but one that led to a dead end. He picked up his phone and talked briefly to his senior deputy. "Listen, I know our check earlier today said that this Bill White character died, but double check on it. Let me know more about him. Also see if he had a twin brother or any relative that looked like him, even if the guy is a little older. And track down his Dad, maybe he looked like him."

It was close to nine in the morning, he wanted to talk. Picking up the phone Sheriff Gibbs dialed my hotel and asked the hotel operator to patch him through to my room. I wasn't there.

Chapter 14

I awoke to the smell of coffee. Actually the sound of the small coffee pot brewing in the room may have been what first got my attention. I sat up and looked over. Sarah was sitting there with a cup of coffee smiling at me.

"You awake, sleeping beauty?" She had a smirk on her face. She brought a cup of coffee over to me, "I guess I wasn't good enough for you to take advantage of last night." Her smirk was still there.

I didn't know how to respond. I knew she was pulling my leg but I hadn't really intended to fall asleep like I had. "I guess I wasn't too exciting last night. Sorry about that, next time you better look out."

She rolled her eyes at me. My pretend threat obviously hadn't scared her. "I need to run," she stated, "I need to go home, get cleaned up, change clothes and get to work. Some of us still pay taxes, you know. As soon as I can break free I'll call you here. If you aren't here I'll leave a note at the desk. You know you are really behind the times, you need to get a cell phone." She walked over and gave me a quick kiss on the lips. As she walked out she looked back and commented how all her friends would be disappointed with her lack of a story about her night in a hotel room with the stranger from out of town.

I knew she was just picking on me but it bothered me a little bit. Since my divorce, I had had only a handful of relationships with women. The divorce had hurt and I simply didn't have the motivation to start a serious relationship. A friend of mine who was a doctor got me talking about my sex life since my marriage fell apart. He told me that what I was going through was not uncommon. It was simply easier to avoid relationships than to develop them. Whether I fully realized it or not, he claimed I was trying to hide or escape from any relationship that could hurt me like my last one. I don't know if I agreed with him completely but I knew he wasn't far off. I felt safe living my life now. And, it was uncomplicated.

I lay there on the bed looking up at the light and tried to assess my feelings. I really had not intended to fall asleep, at least not consciously.

I got up and put on some of the new clothes I purchased the day before. They felt new and stiff and I wished I could have washed them first. I also realized I was dumb not to have gotten some new underwear. I would have to do that as soon as the stores opened. Wanting to get out of the room, I went next door to the pancake house. I felt like a regular there. In fact the waitress brought my coffee to me as soon as I sat down. I told her I only wanted toast and coffee, I needed to think. If I could only get my mind off Sarah, I could probably make some strides on formulating an investigative plan.

After I finished my toast and was on my second cup of coffee, I borrowed a pen from the waitress and started scribbling some thoughts on a napkin. Not very professional I thought. The young kids these days would probably be doing this on a laptop. Sarah was right, I was behind the times. In a few months we would starting a new century. Maybe I would get a cell phone then.

As the waitress was filling my cup up for the third time, I was surprised by Sheriff Gibbs who came to join me at the table. "I called you at your room. The desk told me you came over here. I wanted to discuss something that came up this morning. It may be a dead end but I don't want to leave it at that." Sheriff Gibbs relayed the story he had heard from Mrs. Sattler earlier in the morning. "I have everyone out checking to see if this Billy White character had a brother, a cousin, any relative at all who may have looked like him. You have connections in the military, right?" He asked me, and as I nodded to the affirmative, "When he left here around eighteen years ago he did so to join the Marines. Yet when he drowned a year to two later he was out. Can you find out what may have caused his early discharge?"

"Sure, it may take a day or so. Not much longer though. Let me ask you a question. You say he drowned, did anyone find his body?" It would not have been the first time someone had faked their own death, I thought.

"He was one of three in a crew that disappeared from a boat that was found drifting at sea. All three were missing and assumed drowned. None of the three have ever been seen or heard of since. Just to double check, I ran all three names through a variety of city records today and none of them popped up. If he is here and is alive, he must be using a different name. There are a lot of people who would have known him from those days who are still here. I have my guys interviewing some who knew him best to see if they have seen him or someone who looks like him around." The Sheriff stopped talking and looked at me and then at the napkin I had been writing on.

"You have been moving fast. It is only nine thirty in the morning." I said, perhaps to defend my own lack of progress.

"Mrs. Sattler actually provided the information first to one of my deputies late yesterday. We started our checks at that time. Even if he was alive I don't see a connection with our case, but we are digging there too. It is our only lead to date. What have you got there?" He again was looking at my napkin.

"Not much, I was just diagramming the case and probable relationships. Add in a few assumptions and we get a list of likely leads to pursue. For example, we are assuming the same person killed all our victims and that the killer was known by the victims. I agree with what you said yesterday, that there was likely an emotional attachment of some sort to Annie, our first victim. Maybe the killer was a lover or a rival suitor. The connection with the Fensters was their ability to identify him. The connection to Rick can be much weaker. He could have just stumbled onto the murderer. We assume that he knew something that we didn't, but he may not have. We also know the obvious, that the killer was present here in Denton at the time of the three separate incidents. He could have been gone in between but he obviously had to be here for each of the killings. He seems to be a good shot and uses nine millimeter ammunition. We need to do some link analysis with hotel records, utility records, credit card records, whatever. Long shots, but they should be done. That's about as far as I got before you showed up."

"That's good," Gibbs stated. "We can jump on those

immediately. I agree with what you have laid out."

"If you don't mind Sheriff, I would like to drive down to my place, get some new clothes and return. Don't worry, I'll be back. This case has gotten under my skin, too."

"The case or Sarah?" Gibbs asked with a smile. "I hear you two are now sharing a motel room. You be sweet to her, she is a great kid."

"You would be amazed to hear just how much of a gentleman I have been Sheriff. I'll be back later this evening." By now I knew I shouldn't be surprised at how fast gossip circulated in this town.

He told me to go ahead and reminded me to follow up on White. He gave me White's date of birth to help with the identification. Bill or William White was probably a very common name. We talked a little more and then both left the restaurant.

I walked back to the room wondering if I should call Sarah and tell her I was leaving town or not. I figured that I should. As I entered my room, though, I realized there would be no need to call her. She was sitting on the couch watching television. She looked up at me and smiled, "Rosie at the desk gave me my own key. She thought you wouldn't mind after last night." She giggled at my expense.

"You know I don't think there is a movement I make in this town without everyone knowing it. It is rather amazing." I looked at her, "You are more than welcome to keep that key."

"Thanks," she replied.

"Are you off for the day?" I asked. She said she was, when she arrived at her office her boss had insisted she turn right around and take the day off.

I told her of my plans to drive to my home to grab a few things. "How about coming with me? You can meet my dog and help me pick out some clothes that aren't too old fashioned. We should be back this evening before it gets dark."

"I would love to," she answered. "It would probably do me some good to get out of town for a day, too."

As we walked out to my car, I mentioned to Sarah that I had a conversation with Sheriff Gibbs that morning. I told her of the possible Billy White connection. She could not recall anyone by that name. She had never seen it mentioned in any of the stories on Annie's murder. He would have been about ten years older than her so if he left town after high school to join the Marines, she may have never met him.

"I suggest we ask Marge to see if she could find any old stories that may have mentioned him." She said as we drove out of town.

"Good idea," I concurred.

She called Marge on her cell phone and related our interest in any news she could uncover on an individual named Billy, or possibly William, White. I shared the information about his date of birth with Sarah who passed it on to Marge.

For the first ten or so minutes into the ride through the rain we debated whether or not this Billy White character could be our killer. We acknowledged we were grasping at straws but we had nothing else yet to go on. At least chasing his shadow gave us some momentum. Forensics reports had been coming in but they provided little of value until we had a suspect to check them against.

Once we hit the caprock area of New Mexico we left the rain behind us and our conversation shifted to more personal topics.

"Why after traveling and living all over the world did you end up back in New Mexico?" Sarah asked.

It was an easy conversational subject and I had no problem taking up a good portion of the couple hour drive to Clovis talking about all the factors that drew me back to the southwest. A native of that part of the country herself, she agreed with most of my logic.

"I really liked just about any place I lived or visited all over the world. Asia was fascinating. The cities there teemed with people, packed streets, exotic smells and fascinating places to see. The country side was lush and green and had a lot of vegetation and plants that are somewhat unique to that part of the world. Europe has so much history. The castle, cathedrals, and palaces are simply amazing. You know there are thousands of buildings over there still being used that are older than the United States is as a country."

I looked at her, "Am I rambling on too much?"

"No please go on," she answered smiling.

I went on about the food, beer and wine in Europe.

"How about other places you lived in America?"

"They also have their positive aspects. I loved San Antonio and almost settled there."

We went on discussing the places I had lived. As far as why I settled down back here, it was just that out here in New Mexico, probably like a handful of other western states, a person could really feel free. There were no crowds and little traffic unless you got caught in the heart of one of the few bigger cities during rush hour. The people were friendly and things in general were not nearly as expensive as they are in a lot of our major urban areas.

Conservation efforts in the last half century have allowed many of the native wildlife species to again become common. It was not unusual to see deer, antelope, fox, even the occasional coyote when driving through the country. Armadillo carcasses lined the highways, a macabre proof of their comeback.

Besides, I explained to her, it was always easy to travel somewhere else if I felt the urge to go urban for a while. I hadn't yet, but I admitted it might be nice to go back to New York or even San Antonio for a weekend. Sarah had not been to either and commented that she had heard a lot of nice things about the River Walk in San Antonio.

I had enjoyed living in San Antonio and recommended that she make the trip sometime. She commented that she didn't know anyone there and would probably need a guide to see all the sights. I smiled and told her I might know a good guide that would probably help her out for the right price.

We talked about skiing in New Mexico. The resort areas had become more crowded in recent years and had adapted the higher prices normally found Colorado and California. But still, in our bias, we gave the edge to skiing in New Mexico.

Montana is known as "Big Sky Country" but I often thought New Mexico could have easily shared that moniker. As we drove further south, we left the clouds behind us and the sky turned a beautiful blue. Once past the caprock, the ground flattened and you could see for miles in every direction.

"You know," Sarah commented after a moment of silence,

"if our killer lived out of town in a ranch like one of these, those of us in Denton might not know him very well.   Not these ranches, specifically, as we are kind of far away from Denton, but there are probably hundreds of small ranches within a thirty mile radius of Denton.   Many of the families are active in Denton but there are several who rarely spend anytime in the city."

She paused and then continued, "When I was a teenager, there was a strange girl in my class who we all thought was just weird.   Somehow it came out one day that she had been sexually abused for years by her father. I believe he was her step-father. She was removed from the house and I believe her step-father went to jail. My parents discussed this one evening after the trial was over and I remember my mother saying that it was no wonder that he could get away with it so long. She said these ranches were like the castles of the middle ages, what happened inside their walls no one knew but the rancher. The neighbors are too far away to hear anything and unless the rancher is friendly, you need a warrant just to get close to the ranch house. I'm sure such abuse happens inside a city, too, but Mom's point was valid."

"Her perception of the privacy of some of these ranches was right on." I added. "Very rarely do you hear of some crazy religious cult setting up their compound in the middle of a city. They almost always find someplace out in the country where they can have and keep their privacy." I paused for a moment, "Rick was north of town a few miles when he was murdered. Obviously somebody from town could have met him out there but it is more likely he was out there in search of someone or to meet someone who was already there."

"It does not seem likely that someone from town would want to drive out of town to meet with Rick since he works in town himself." She hesitated, "I mean worked in town."

We drove on in silence for a few minutes. I decided to change the subject and asked her if she had ever visited Clovis. She said she had been there a few times, both for rodeos when she was younger and with her high school crowd to watch a football game. She liked Clovis. It was a little bigger than Denton and had a few more things to do. I chuckled to myself as I thought of Clovis as a fairly small, sleepy town. Most residents thought that if the local Air Base, Cannon Air Force Base, located just west of the city closed down, that Clovis, itself, would just fade away. I didn't really buy their logic but I acknowledged the base closure would have a severe impact.

"Who has been taking care of your dog?" she asked as we approached my neighborhood.

"Chubs," I responded, "is being taken care of by my neighbors. My back door has a small pet door that Chubs uses to get in and out. I left him with enough water and food for one day. The first evening, when I realized I would not be getting home I called them and asked them to cover for me. They have two teen age daughters who love Chubs and I am sure they are spoiling him a lot more than I ever could."

"Well I am looking forward to meeting this Chubs of yours. What kind of dog is it?"

"A mix of a mix of dogs is the way I like to put it. I'm not sure what exactly is in him. But he is a good dog. Small to medium sized and very friendly. Chubs was given to me by a friend whose own dog had a litter of unwanted pups and he simply couldn't give them all away. I told him I didn't want one either, but he and his wife insisted. It was shortly after my divorce. I guess they thought they were doing something nice. I really didn't want it but I have to confess, Chubs has grown on me over time."

We pulled into my driveway.

"Nice house," Sarah remarked. "It looks a lot bigger than mine."

I took her in through the front door, thinking that would give her a better impression than going through the garage. My attempt to impress her was immediately interrupted though by Chubs who proceeded to repeatedly bark and run back and forth in front of us.

"I believe his rude behavior is simply a combination of telling me he is mad I left him alone for so long and to tell you this is his house and until he has approved of you he is going to be keeping an eye on you." I said with a smile.

"We can fix that," Sarah replied. She kneeled down and extended her hand towards Chubs who immediately sniffed it and let her rub his head and ears. He immediately calmed down, obviously deciding that Sarah was okay.

"I am starting to believe you have that affect on all males."

She smiled back up at me as if to say you haven't seen anything yet.

I smiled back. "Make yourself at home, there are soft drinks in the refrigerator or feel free to make some coffee. I want to run next door and talk to the Hunters for a minute."

I was back in less than five minutes. The Hunters had no

problem with continuing to watch Chubs. Their own dog and Chubs got along well and together they always got a lot of exercise.

"Sarah," I called when I entered my house. She was nowhere to be seen. I looked in the kitchen and the den. I heard a bark out back and walked to the back door. She was out back throwing a Frisbee with Chubs.

"I don't believe it," I shouted out the back door. "Is he actually bringing the Frisbee back to you? He never does that for me." Actually, Chubs sometimes did, but not that often and I thought it wouldn't hurt to keep Sarah's spirits up.

"Chubs is a good boy, aren't you Chubs?" Sarah responded as she scratched him behind his ears. "And, he is so handsome." Chubs seemed to understand her and stood up posing on his hind legs.

"He is a ham, don't let him kid you." I stated, but I was happy they were getting along. I suddenly realized everything I was doing or saying was motivated by my desire to strengthen our relationship. Just as quickly, I started having the same old doubts that I have had for years now. I figured I was headed for quite an emotional struggle. My subconscious and conscious mind were not about to give in to my heart. Frustrated, I walked back to my bedroom still not really knowing for which side of myself I was rooting.

Sarah was sweet and pretty, but I was a dozen years older than her, maybe more. We were both single but she undoubtedly looked at relationships with youthful optimism and dreams. I didn't want to look at relationships like that anymore. She was still growing and experimenting. I had seen enough and didn't want to go back into life's chemistry lab. She probably would want to get married and have kids. I wouldn't. She would go into the relationship with the courage to make it work. I was starting to realize I had become an emotional coward.

I quickly changed clothes, including underwear and packed one suitcase. When I came back out to the kitchen, I found Sarah and Chubs snacking on some peanut butter cookies. "These are good," Sarah said, "I hope you don't mind my sharing them with Chubs. He seems to really like them."

"I don't mind at all. Other than those things that are harmful, like chicken bones, I let him have whatever he wants. Saves on dog food. He especially likes pastrami sandwiches."

"I'll make us all sandwiches, if you want," Sarah offered.

"I wish you could but I don't think I have enough bread or any pastrami for that matter. But there is a good restaurant just down the road and I'll be happy to buy you some lunch."

"You should have told me you have a pool, I would have brought my bathing suit."

"If you behave," I teased, "maybe I'll bring you back some time." With a wink, I continued. "Besides, if you really want to swim, you could borrow one of my suits."

"I'm afraid your suit would be too big for me," she said, getting her own barb back at me. "Let's go eat."

It was only a five minute drive to the restaurant. La Fiesta was one of my favorites and the owner and staff knew me well. Elena, the head waitress, who also happened to own the restaurant with her husband, immediately came over to us and asked us for our order. She teased me about my lousy tipping habits and said that she hoped to remember what I ordered this time. She and Sarah seemed to hit it off.

Shortly after we sat down, Sarah excused herself to use the restroom. I noticed that after she came out of the restroom, Elena made some comment to her and the two of them started talking by the cashier's counter. They chatted for nearly ten minutes occasionally giggling and glancing at me. I was getting a bit irritated and made a mental note to give Elena even a more miserly tip than normal.

When Sarah finally returned, I couldn't help but ask, "What was that all about?"

"You," she said with a smile. "You should have told me Elena knew you so well."

"She doesn't," was my response. "Elena is a friend and that is all. She is married and our relationship, for the most past, has existed here in the restaurant and at an occasional encounter at some function we both have found ourselves attending."

I didn't see any need to tell Sarah about the time I had helped Elena's cousin out of a nasty situation. It had solidified my friendship with Elena but was something I needed to keep buried for my own protection.

I had barely known Elena at the time of the incident and had only been back in New Mexico a couple of months. I had been wrangled into participating in a five kilometer charity walk by a "so-called friend" who overslept and missed the walk himself. About half way through the walk I found myself walking just in front of Elena and her cousin who ran a restaurant, similar to Elena's, in Portales, a nearby town.

The two cousins were talking in earnest and to my surprise

were crying. I asked them if I could do anything to help and they both clammed up after telling me no. After the event, and after her cousin had left, Elena approached me and apologized for their behavior on the walk.   We talked some and she explained that her cousin was being squeezed by two local gangs, each wanting a percentage of the restaurant's income. Her cousin's husband had been assaulted by one of the gangs and they were both afraid to approach the police for help.

Elena didn't ask for my help, nor did I commit to anything. I just told her that maybe I could help out a little behind the scenes. She looked at me doubtfully and we never again discussed the matter.

After my discussion with Elena I talked to a couple of contacts with the Roosevelt County Sheriff's office. I confirmed that two rival gangs had recently emerged in the county and were now competing for dominance.   Both were loosely affiliated with factions within the Mexican mafia. Local police efforts had been able to retard the gangs' growth but had not been able to seriously cripple them.

I ended up talking to a young city cop who was able to show me the main characters in the two gangs, the primary vehicles they used and some of their hang outs. The police knew the gangs were heavy into the protection rackets but couldn't get any of the victims to formally file a complaint.

It took a couple weeks of surveillance before I came up with my plan. It all depended on timing and stealth on my part. A primary collector for one of the gangs ran his route every Wednesday morning. One of his stops was a dry cleaner on Main and another, just about fifty yards up the street, was a small restaurant where he would spend a few extra minutes flirting with a waitress. He had a briefcase on the passenger seat of his small Toyota that he put the pay-offs in as he went along. He never carried the briefcase in and out of the car and the only spot where he left it unattended for more than the time to go into a place and collect a payment was in front of the cleaners on Main.

I watched him go into and come out of the dry cleaners. He went immediately to his car to deposit the payment into the briefcase and then headed up to the restaurant. As soon as the collector stepped into the restaurant, I was at the street side door to his car and had it popped open. The briefcase, as I expected, was chained to the seat. Rather than worry about the chain I had brought along a tool to cut through the briefcase handle. It took less than five seconds.

Next, I was out of the car with the briefcase and walking diagonally across the street and through a parking lot that separated the south bound Main Street from the northbound section of the same road. My target there was an old white pickup truck belonging to a member of the opposing gang. The truck was parked in front of a small local coffee shop where a few members of this gang hung out almost every weekday morning.

I tossed the briefcase in through the truck's open window and veered back towards the Toyota. I got back with a few minutes to spare and was able to intercept the collector, stopping him just as he got to his Toyota. In my role as a good citizen, I told him I had just seen some guy taking something out of his car and running over to an old white pickup across the road. I pointed out the pickup to him as we could barely see it from his car.

The collector looked in his car and saw the briefcase was gone. Cursing he started running towards the pickup truck I had pointed out, without so much as a thank you to me. I waited until he was just about to the truck and, using a pay phone next door to the dry cleaners, called the coffee shop to let them know someone was breaking into a white pickup parked in front of their building.

What happened next was much more than I expected. Three goons from the coffee shop gang came out and attacked the collector while he was getting into their car. Outnumbered the collector pulled a knife and was promptly gunned down. The three gang members then jumped into the white pickup and sped off. The briefcase was still in the pickup.

The collector's bullet wound was not fatal and he was on his cell phone reporting in to his gang before the pickup was out of sight. A quick and furious gang war ensued that afternoon. By the time the police finally got everything under control, fourteen gang bangers were arrested for felony weapons and assault charges. Three were dead and most of the surviving had suffered some serious injury. On the bright side, both gangs were neutered and quickly faded away.

I never told anyone about my involvement. The only thing I couldn't resist was a quick stop by Elena's restaurant the evening everything went down and as I was getting my three tacos to go mentioned to her that I thought everything might be turning out all right for her cousin.

She didn't understand me then but later, after she heard the news of the two gangs being put out of business, asked me how I knew. I told her was that I had a few friends that kept me informed and left it at that. She never asked me again about it.

Sarah and I spent the next hour eating and having a nice conversation about food and restaurants. By the time we left and started driving back to Denton, the stormy weather had reached Clovis. Our drive back was not going to be as quick as the one down.

Shortly after we left the city limits and headed directly into the rain, Sarah leaned over and rested her head against the window. I thought she was tired and was going to sleep. We rode along in silence.

Sarah, however, was not tired. She was absorbed in thought. She told me later that Elena had been blunt and to the point. At first, this had surprised her and she thought Elena was being rude. But just as suddenly, she realized that Elena meant well. The information she passed on had answered a lot of questions that she had already been asking herself.

Sarah thought to herself that she certainly didn't expect every man she went out with to try to score on the first date, but, as she told me later, I was not behaving like any other man she had known. She had dropped enough hints and had given me enough opportunities to make a move. A move she wanted to happen, but I hadn't tried anything. She started to question herself. Elena's information had resolved all that. It also allowed her to begin plotting, yes that was a good word she thought with a smile, plotting a new course of action to take to get through the dumb defenses that I had put up around my emotions.

Elena had taken the opportunity to talk to Sarah, because as she said, it was obvious that there was some chemistry between Sarah and me. "I know it may be none of my business," Elena had started the conversation with Sarah, "but can I talk to you for a second about Jim?" Although I didn't realize it until much later, she had gone on to tell Sarah about the many women who had made a move on me in the past couple of years, just to run into a stone wall. Elena provided her theory as to why I behaved the way I do, which happened to be pretty accurate. She then provided Sarah a few suggestions on how she would handle the challenge if she was single. Sarah thanked her and took her suggestions to heart.

Rather than resting her mind, Sarah was letting it race with thoughts. The last thing on her mind as we drove back towards Denton was the murder investigation we had found ourselves in the middle.

On the other hand, that was exactly what had filtered back into my own thoughts. I should have called my old contacts at the FBI first thing this morning but it had slipped my mind. I would have to do it as soon as we got back to Denton. I was hoping it wouldn't be too late in D.C. Over the years I had developed a good friend at the FBI who I thought would still pass information to me.

As luck would have it we were only a dozen or so miles from Denton when we were stopped at a road block by the state highway patrol. Although the rain had tapered off to a steady drizzle, the heavy rains from earlier in the day had caused a small creek to overflow its banks. Water was running across a dip in the road making it too dangerous for vehicles to cross.

Sarah sat upright as we came to a stop. The patrolman walked over and told us that a tractor was on its way to try to divert the water back off the road. He thought just a foot or two of dirt along the thirty foot stretch of road might do the trick. Looking at the steady rush of water, I was not nearly as optimistic.

I considered heading back and trying to find a different route. However, I figured any small country road, many of them not even paved, would have similar flooding problems and an alternate paved route would take nearly an hour. I decided to stay and hope the tractor could save the day. Unfortunately it was not yet in sight.

Sarah took out her cell phone and asked whether we should check in with the Sheriff. I asked her if he had her cell number. She wasn't sure but thought he could easily get it from the office if he wanted it.

"Then there is probably no reason to call him," I commented. "Could I use your phone to track down some information for the Sheriff. I'll reimburse you." Sarah stated that she would remember the offer and handed me the phone. I had to dig into my wallet to find the card I still carried with me. Pete Riley had been with the FBI for over twenty years. I first met him when he was assigned to the U.S. Embassy in Madrid as the LEGAT (Legal Attaché). Since then our paths had crossed a few more times and we had become good friends.

Luck was with us. I reached Pete on my first attempt. He was happy to hear from me and we chatted about our current lives for a few minutes before getting to business. Like most of my friends he wanted to make sure I was surviving as a bachelor and asked whether or not I had found a new bride.

They always thought they were being either cute or helpful, I didn't know which, but I found such conversation just rekindled the hurt. He told me he had a sister-in-law with good teeth and strong bones who would be just right for me. In jest, I told him that I would be interested in reading her bio and seeing a set of pictures. He told me not to be surprised if they showed up in the mail in the next week. The gal was desperate.

We finally got down to business on the phone. I told Pete of my interest into a guy named Bill White and gave him White's date of birth. We chatted some more about his family while he pulled White up on the computer.

"The FBI's record on him is fairly sparse. No arrests or convictions and he was not a subject of any FBI file. But I have a cross reference to both the Navy and the North Carolina State Police. That usually indicates they have additional relevant information. If you want to dig deep you will have to contact them. I can give you contacts at both if you need them." Pete passed on the names and phone numbers to both. "By the way," he continued, "you haven't seen any aliens out there in New Mexico have you? Little green men from outer space, not the ones from south of the border. We have had a number of people just disappear from the face of the earth in the past couple of years and my bet is that what ever is happening to them is happening in New Mexico."

I knew he was just pulling my leg with the reference to men from outer space. New Mexico was infamous for the Roswell incident and other stories relating to visitors from space. "How are they disappearing and why do you think it is happening in New Mexico?"

"Well, Jim, this is mostly my theory, although I have a lot of supporters here. About a dozen individuals traveling across the country, either by hitchhiking or illegally catching rides on trains, have simply disappeared. We have had a major task force working it for some time without any success. Despite thousands of interviews and the help of a number of local and state agencies we have not come up with any trace of any of the missing. The best I can piece it together, almost all of the victims disappeared while in the vicinity of New Mexico along the I-40 corridor."

'That corridor runs all the way across the state and when you say vicinity I guess you mean part of Texas and Arizona?" I asked.

"You are correct, buddy. That is our real dilemma. We don't have a definite fix on any of them. Many of these people travel alone. Everyone knows hitchhiking is dangerous but people still do it. Sneaking illegally onto a freight train can be just as dangerous. As you know, there are a lot of predators out there. You know of any Jane or John Does popping up dead out there?"

"No I sure don't," I responded. "I'll ask around and let you know if I hear anything though." We both knew that he was likely to hear something long before I would as most local agencies report the discovery of unidentified dead bodies to state and federal authorities. But he sounded as though he was grasping at straws and I was happy to be one for him.

After hanging up, I turned to Sarah, who had been listening to my conversation with Pete Riley. "Not too much help," I said. "But he did give me some other contacts, do you mind?" I held up her phone gesturing I would like to make another call.

"It will cost you," was her response.

I figured I could pay the bill and dialed the number to the North Carolina State Police.   I was able to get through to Lieutenant Roger Moore. After telling him who I was and my being referred to him by Pete Riley from the FBI, Lieutenant Moore offered his assistance. As I had done with Riley, I passed on Bill White's name and date of birth to Moore. This time I was also able to provide his social security number as I had obtained that from Riley. Moore asked me if I wanted to wait on hold while he pulled up the information his databases had on White. I told him I would wait.

"I'm on hold," I mentioned to Sarah, "I hope these things aren't that expensive. I'll have to take on a second job."

"I'm keeping track. A new fur coat would come in handy this winter." She smiled. I wasn't too sure if she was kidding.

It wasn't much longer and Moore came back on the phone. "Can I ask you what your interest is in this character, Mr. West?"

"I know it's a long shot, Lieutenant, but we have had a couple of unsolved murders out here in Denton, New Mexico, and his name has come up. I know he is supposed to be dead but his name is the only lead we have at this time."

"Fascinating," responded Moore, "if you actually put your hands on this guy, let us know immediately. He was a lead subject in a shooting murder of a Marine Sergeant before he disappeared. He was believed to have drowned with two other individuals in a boating mishap, however, his body was never found. Not any of the three bodies were ever found. We had every trace in the world out looking for anything that might pop up on White after the accident but nothing ever did. The records allude to a theory some of the folks here had back then that he might have used the boating incident to cover his tracks and make his escape, but we never uncovered a shred of evidence to substantiate that theory. Officially we have him listed as dead and as such there are no outstanding warrants."

"Can you fax or e-mail a copy of everything you have to Sheriff Gibbs in Denton, New Mexico. It may help us and we will certainly let you know if we discover anything else."

He said he would and asked if I would pass on Gibbs' office phone number so he could confirm with them the best way to transmit the information. I thought it may also be a subtle way to double check who he was actually sending it to, but that was fine.

"One more," I said to Sarah and dialed the number to the Naval Criminal Investigative Service that Riley had provided. This elite group of federal investigators handled all serious felony investigations in the Navy, and that included those that occurred within the Marine Corps. I had a lot of friends in the Navy and could have gone straight to one of them. I decided to use Riley's contact as I could always use an additional networking contact and, in the off chance the two of them chatted in the future, I wanted to make sure they both knew I closed the loop. It turned out the Navy did not have anything more than the State Police had. White couldn't make it in the Marines and was discharged early. He was a lead suspect in the murder of the same Sergeant who had been instrumental in his discharge. As the incident did not happen on a military installation and the prime suspect was a civilian, the Navy had been dependent on the local authorities who were in charge of the investigation.

After I hung up, Sarah asked, "Are we wasting our time pursuing a dead man?"

"We may be, but if he wasn't believed to be dead, his possible involvement in all of this would have been investigated. He was also the prime suspect in a murder that happened over a decade ago in North Carolina. Combine that with the information that Luke's grandmother mentioned his name a day or so before she died and we have set of coincidences that we simply can not overlook."

"Why doesn't anyone else know he is in town? He had to have friends back then who would recognize him even now," Sarah remarked.

"As of this morning, no one has tried to track down all his friends. I think that is what the Sheriff is doing right now. Until we get a better lead, pursuing this alleged dead guy may be the best way to get to resolution on this case." I knew I was trying to convince myself, as much as Sarah, that our focus on White was logical. He could easily be dead, but I had learned long ago not to ignore anomalies that pop up in a case that link a suspect to more than one unrelated but similar crime. Maybe this dead man could still kill.

"Sorry about this delay," I mentioned to Sarah, referring to our being stuck on the highway.

"It is certainly not your fault," she responded. "Besides, I think I see the tractor coming right now."

The rain had totally stopped and the water running across

the road was looking shallower. "Better late than never," I remarked with a smile.

The tractor looked to me like a road grader, but I guess it could have been a tractor with a grader attached to the front of it. Not being an expert on heavy machinery I didn't say anything. The tractor made quick work of the overflow, pushing a large mound of dirt to the side of the road that edged the creek bed. Within just a few minutes the water that was overflowing onto the road was diverted back to the main flow that ran along side the road to the deeper creek bed about two hundred yards ahead and crossed the road harmlessly under a small bridge.

We were finally allowed to continue on our way to Denton. Despite the delay, there were only a handful of cars backed up behind us when were allowed to drive on to Denton. Within fifteen minutes we were there.

"Where to?" I asked Sarah.

"To the Sheriff's office. Let's see if he has developed anything new. Hopefully something has popped up."

We pulled up in front of the sheriff's office and went inside. Gibbs was in and appeared happy we were back. Unfortunately, despite an intense canvassing of everyone who may have known Bill White in the past, no one had seen or heard from him since he had joined the Marines.

That information was disheartening as it seemed improbable he could be living in the area or even just come into town on an occasional basis and not be seen or recognized. I passed along the information I had obtained by phone and Gibbs acknowledged he had already received the fax from North

Carolina. We agreed that the link to a prior homicide was a significant coincidence, but only if he were alive and here in New Mexico. So far, nothing we had developed added any credence to those two possibilities. We spent a few minutes discussing what leads we may have ignored because of our focus on White and came up without any better ideas to spend our time in the immediate future.

"I would like to go back and bounce what we have off Tony, my editor, and maybe a few others. They may have some ideas for us. Would that be okay?" Sarah asked.

"As long as you can insure they understand not to print anything yet," instructed the Sheriff. "We are not ready to go prime time on this. I know Tony won't do anything rash, I just need to make sure he understands our position."

"That will be no problem at all," Sarah replied. As with many small towns, the relationship between the law and the press was close. The Sheriff and courts routinely shared information early with the local paper and for the paper's part, they rarely published anything relating to an ongoing case without some form of informal coordination. This was nothing close to censorship, just a good understanding of each others' equities based on a foundation of trust. It was a bond not found in most big cities and almost never at the national level.

We discussed the case a little bit longer. Sheriff Gibbs gave me a copy of the faxed report from the North Carolina State Police. Shortly thereafter Sarah and I left. It was late in the afternoon. I offered to buy Sarah some dinner, but she declined saying that she wanted to spend some time at the office. She said she would check in later in the evening. I drove her back to her car and dropped her off. Clouds seemed to be gathering again in the horizon and it looked as though the rain might return.

I returned to the hotel. It was beginning to feel like home. I wanted to start working on another theory of mine.

Chapter 15

Sarah spent about an hour at the offices of her newspaper. She discussed the status of the investigation with her editor. Although extremely interested, he was not able to shed any light on the dilemma that faced them or come up with any good ideas to pursue. He agreed the paper should keep a lid on the story for the time being. Prior to going home, Sarah gave Marge a call at the archives.

"You just caught me, Sarah. I was walking out the door. What can I do for you?"Marge asked as she was gathering up her things from her desk. This was her night for bingo at the VFW hall. It was usually crowded and Marge wanted to get there early enough to secure her favorite table.

"Marge, I need you to do some sleuthing for me. A person, a Billy or Bill White keeps coming up in our case. He used to live here over nearly twenty years ago and then he went off to join the Marines. No one has seen or heard of him since. In fact, he may actually be dead. I am interested in anyone who may have seen or heard from him in the past couple of years or who may know where he is now. Actually we are interested in anything anybody can tell us about him. Don't let on why you are interested Marge. We don't want to start any rumors. Just dig a little with your contacts."

Marge asked a few questions of Sarah to better identify who Bill White was and then told her she would see what she could uncover. If she learned anything she would pass it on to Sarah.

Sarah checked her desks for any notes and glanced at her e-mails. Everything was routine and could wait until later. It was getting dark when she walked out to her car. She actually had not wanted to have dinner alone. But her thoughts had been with Elena's advice to her.

Elena had been trying to be helpful. "Sarah," she had said after the two were alone, "please forgive me if I am out of line, but if you are interested in Jim you need to appreciate the challenges you are going to face. Many women have tried to capture his heart since he has come to live here. None have succeeded. Probably because they all tried to move too quickly. I know him fairly well. We talk. If I wasn't married to the old goat I have as a husband, I would try for his heart. You need to take it slow with Jim. He still hurts from his divorce. Don't be too aggressive. Give him time to make up his own mind. One or two women here were more patient and they had the most success with him, but in the end they failed, too." They talked further, but it was this advice that prompted Sarah to skip dinner. She also needed some time to herself. Too much had happened in a few short days and she needed some time to get her thoughts together. She also needed to figure out this man who had somehow, in just a couple of days, crept so quickly into her heart.

Sarah stopped briefly at an Albertsons grocery store to get a few items before continuing on her way home. When she finally pulled into her driveway, she wished she had left a light on somewhere. The nearest street light was not far away but its light was partially blocked by a tall, old oak in her neighbor's yard. There was still enough light left to fumble with her keys and unlock her front door. A sudden noise behind her startled her. She spun around in a panic. It was just an empty paper bag blowing down the street.

She stepped into her home and turned on the lights. The quietness of the house only added to her jitters. She bolted the door behind her. Telling herself it was silly to let fear affect her so, she made herself walk from room to room turning on the lights and ensuring she was alone. She was. Finally, she looked out a window to her front yard and, with a little more apprehension, a back window to survey her back yard. Everything looked fine and Sarah began to calm down.

Suddenly Sarah wished she had brought Chubs back to Denton with her. A watch dog, even a small one, would certainly be comforting right now. Maybe she needed to get a dog of her own. She had always liked pets, but she figured with her job she simply couldn't give a pet the attention it needed. Maybe she would have to reconsider that decision.

She put a can of minestrone soup in a pot, added half the recommended water and placed it on the stove. Not much of a supper, she admitted to herself, but she had done quite a lot of eating lately and was going to go light tonight. She was blessed with a good figure but like most women, she wasn't totally satisfied with her appearance.

The inside of Sarah's house was as simple as the outside. She did not have any ornate furniture. In fact, not all of the rooms even had furniture. One of the three bedrooms was empty with the exception of a few boxes she stored in the room. She had nicely furnished the master bedroom which she used as her bedroom. In one of the other two bedrooms she had some basics for any guests that came to visit her. The dining room had a nice table and chairs, but nothing else. In her mind, furnishing a house was something she would get into after she was married. For now, just the essentials and perhaps a few frills were all that were needed.

When the soup was ready, she poured it into a large mug and carried it into the bathroom. She started the bath water and got undressed as the tub filled and the soup cooled. Looking at herself in the mirror, her thoughts returned to the events of the past few days. The killings were so horrible. Because of them, however, a man had come into her life. She wondered if she was emotionally sick or was flawed in some other way. Was it wrong to have allowed such strong emotions and personal gratification to grow out of such a tragedy? Could she actually be happy that these terrible killings had occurred just so she could have met and fallen so hard for a man she had not even known just a few days earlier.

The dilemma troubled her. If somehow she now had the ability to prevent the killings from ever happening in the first place, would she do so? Even if it meant she would have never gotten to know Jim West? As she settled into the bath water, she reluctantly admitted to herself that if she had the power, she would have prevented the murders. But, she imagined with a smile, if she had that kind of power she would be able to find some other way to meet Jim. Maybe, she chuckled to herself, even manipulate his troubled heart a little faster.

Chapter 16

What Sarah couldn't realize was that her good fortune was also a factor of another couple's misfortune. Bill's preoccupation with his two house guests delayed his efforts to silence Sarah.

Tiffany Grace had come out of her drug induced stupor slowly. That she had blacked out was not a shock to her as she was a frequent user of a variety of drugs and alcohol. Tiffany had been too wild for her parents to handle since she was fifteen. She was not evil or mean by any stretch of the definition, she just never understood the relevance of morality when it came to her own personal behavior. Life had just come too free and easy for her.

She had come out of a drunken or drug induced unconsciousness many times before. Frequently in surroundings she didn't recognize. Her friends had told her she was playing with danger but she ignored them. She felt like she had a power over men and could control them. She always had before. What was troubling her now though, as she was struggling to get a hold on her senses, was the nagging realization that she had not done anything this time to cause the way she felt.

Tiffany had started hopping rides on trains just a few months before with a group of people she had met one night at a party. A couple she had met for the first time had claimed to have traveled the country illegally by trains and explained how they did it. Five of the party attendees agreed to meet the next day and together illegally catch a train ride to a town just twenty miles away. That first experience had led to other short trips around the state.

Eventually, she had paired up with Jeff Blight as her train jumping partner. Jeff wasn't the brightest guy she had ever met, nor was he by any means rich, but he was good at sex and obedient and these were two things that Tiffany looked for most in her male companions. After some practice and coaching from the couple they had met at the party, Tiffany and Jeff had embarked on their journey to Hollywood. Their new friends had even given them a makeshift map pointing out the easiest places across the country to get off and back on a train.

The faint sound of a television was the first thing she heard. Then it was gone. Next she thought she heard someone talking to her. She was cold but she didn't know why. She heard a moaning sound next to her that startled her. As she finally regained her consciousness, she realized she was chained by her hands to the ceiling. Her feet were on the ground, but just barely. Her head and arms were aching. She was completely naked.

Hanging just two or three feet from her to her left was Jeff. He too was nude but he was hanging upside down from his feet. His hands were tied behind him. His head was just off the floor. He seemed to still be unconscious.

The small room was empty except for a table that sat off to the side in front of her and a stool. Tiffany noticed that there was a standard metal tool box on the table. She could not see a door or a window. She tried to turn her head around to see what was behind her. She thought she caught sight of a door but nothing else. A pain shot through her neck, shoulders and head when she tried to look around.

The walls looked blotched and stained. Someone had scrubbed them but you could still see the patches that weren't quite white. Tiffany didn't want to even imagine what caused the discoloration. She also didn't like what she saw on the floor. Not a rug, but rather dark brown linoleum that had large dark stains. The stains seemed to be centered under Tiffany's feet and Jeff's head. Terror began to kick in and Tiffany began trembling. She began softly but fervently calling Jeff's name. Jeff was still too much under the influence of the drug to hear her, but someone else did.

The door behind her made a squeaking noise when it swung open. Bill liked the sound of the door as he loved its effect on those he had kept in the room. At the sound of the door he could see them visibly stiffen and, over time, even start whimpering or convulsing in fear. Although shaken, Tiffany had not yet reached that level of terror and tried to turn to see who if anyone was entering the room. Again, a pain shot through her neck and shoulders. She wondered if her shoulder had been dislocated.

"Who are you? What do you want with us?" Tiffany shouted. There was no reply. "We don't have much money, you can have it all. If you want sex, you certainly don't have to chain me up for that. Why are you doing this?" Suddenly a sharp pain shot through Tiffany's lower back in the area of her right kidney, then her left kidney and again on her right.

Tiffany's body instinctively recoiled in pain.

Bill smiled to himself. He had often thought that over the years he had sharpened his boxing skills by using his victims as real live punching dummies. He had also learned where his punches resulted in the most pain. The kidneys were perfect targets. Not only could his victims not see the punch coming, the excruciating pain would produce a psychological impact on his victims every time they heard the door open behind them. But this was just one of dozens of tactics Bill had used to totally break his many victims.

While Tiffany hung there sobbing and trembling, Bill looked over at his male victim. He was still unconscious. It would be more fun when both were awake and could watch. He hoped the male would regain consciousness. He said nothing to the girl and backed out the door closing it behind him.

As he went upstairs out of the basement, Bill wondered if he should turn his attention to Sarah. He decided not to as it was still daylight outside and he was reluctant to leave the two alone. They could go nowhere he was sure, but he wanted to be there when the guy came out of his drugged stupor. His own excitement was starting to build as he anticipated the many hours he would have enjoying the company of his prisoners.

It wasn't too long before he started hearing his male victim shouting obscenities from the basement. He had once wondered if he should wire the basement for sound. However he decided there was no need as when his victims first came to, they inevitably started shouting to be set free. Some of them kept shouting until he responded. Needless to say, most of them stopped shouting after he spent a little time with them.

Bill got up and turned off the television. He went to his room and stripped down. He learned long ago that there was no need to ruin good clothes. He walked quietly down to the basement and pushed the door open. At the sound of the door opening the girl instantly stiffened, but the male continued to curse him and demand to be let down. Hanging upside down he was better able to turn his head around. When he saw Bill standing there nude and smiling, Jeff Blight instantly shut up. Within seconds he began talking to Bill in what seemed to be an easy going manner. This pretense of calmness was brought on by Jeff's instant realization that he was in real danger.

"Say, man, what is going on? We have no real money and very little else to offer you. Why don't you just let us go?" Jeff pleaded.

Bill said nothing in return. He walked around in front of his two prisoners.

Tiffany was hit by two immediate reactions. On the one hand the whole scene seemed like a crazy dream. On the other, she instinctively knew it wasn't only the scene that was utterly crazy, but also this horrible, naked man that stood in front of them.

Bill stared smiling at the two, saying nothing. He would start on the man first and just mess with the young lady enough to keep her attention, he thought. It would do her good just to watch for a while. She would know she would be next.

Reaching into the tool box he removed a heavy duty, battery operated drill that had a thin drill bit attached to it. It was the most powerful cordless one Bill could find in Denton and it had proven very effective. He walked up to the man and around to his back. He turned on the drill and stabbed it into the man's calf. As Jeff screamed in terror and pain, Bill removed the drill bit and stabbed him again behind the knee. To Jeff it was as though someone had lit his nerves on fire. All he could do was scream. Tiffany who could just see what was happening echoed Jeff's screams with her own. Bill repeated the stabs until he had put about six holes in the back of Jeff's legs.

He then walked around in front of the two. Bill's hands and forearms were splattered with blood. The drill was totally covered. He walked up to Tiffany and stood only inches away from her. She stopped screaming and stared at him terrified. He smiled and raised the drill and turned it on. Blood instantly sprayed everywhere, some of it landed on her face. Tiffany cringed backward as Bill lowered the drill bit and then slammed it directly into her arm pit. Tiffany recoiled in pain. Bill pulled the bit out of her and walked back to the table.

Reaching into the tool box again, Bill pulled out a short length of fishing line. He then pulled out a hook that was about an inch long and fastened it to one end of the fishing line. Bill reached back into tool kit and pulled out a second hook of similar size and tied it to the other end of the line. Walking up to Tiffany he reached out and grabbed a large piece of skin on the back of her arm. With some effort he stuck the sharp end of the hook through the flesh. Tiffany screamed and kicked out at Bill repeatedly with her feet. Bill just ignored her flailing. He stepped behind her and gave the line a sharp tug. Again Tiffany screamed and started cursing her tormentor. Bill reached over and grabbed Jeff's leg nearest Tiffany. With some effort he forced the hook at the other end of the line into Jeff's inner thigh. Jeff involuntarily recoiled from the pain causing the hook to go deeper into his leg and violently jerk Tiffany's arm.

Bill went back in front of them and for the first time started talking. "You two can really say you are hooked on each other now." He laughed at his humor. "Hey big guy, if you don't want to hurt your lady friend, you better stop jerking around like a baby."

"Did you know I have a tattoo collection? Let me show it to you." Opening a drawer on the far side of the table, Bill pulled out a scrap book. He opened to the first page and showed it to both of his prisoners. On the page was what looked like an old piece of cloth with a dark print on it. Whatever it was, it was unrecognizable to Tiffany. She looked at Jeff, but he seemed to be in a state of shock. His eyes were pointed towards the ground and there was a trail of drool running from his mouth to the floor.

"Oh, here is a better one," continued Bill as he thumbed through the scrapbook. He opened to a page that contained a very large section of dried skin with a very colorful dragon tattoo. He showed it to Tiffany. "It took a long time to peel this off without damaging it. I had to go out and buy a special knife just to do it." Again, Bill smiled. His eyes seemed to look right through Tiffany.

"I don't have any tattoos you pervert." In the back of her mind she was grateful that she had not fallen for that current fad. "Listen, wouldn't you rather just take me to your bedroom? I'll do anything you want. I can probably even teach you a few things. Just take me down from here and remove this hook." Tiffany tried hard to stay cool and be as seductive as she could. She had thought there was no man alive who could resist her when she was at her best. But she had no impact whatsoever on Bill.

"You will do anything I want, wherever I want, whenever I want. Just wait and see." Bill stated very matter-of-factly to Tiffany.

He then grinned and looked over at Jeff. "He has a nice chain tattoo that circles his entire right arm."

Bill kicked Jeff in his face, not so much to hurt him but to get his attention. Jeff had been babbling and only semi-conscious. He snapped out of his daze and looked up at Bill. There was terror and hate in Jeff's eyes.

Bill leaned down and talked like a parent to a child. "Listen, man, when you jerk around you hurt this young lady here. Every time you move your leg, you cause that hook to pull on her arm. You don't want to hurt your friend do you? So you stay real still while I remove that ugly tattoo from your arm." This was the first time Jeff realized what Bill was threatening to do. As Bill finished speaking he brought his surgeon's scalpel close to Jeff's face and showed it to him. Jeff again started shouting and jerking around frantically trying to free himself. He stopped nearly as fast as he started as the hook in his leg dug deeper and Tiffany shouted in pain.

In terror Jeff hung as still as he could. However, when the scalpel dug into his arm he involuntarily jumped in pain. Within seconds he had totally lost control and violently reacted to each slice through his arm. Shortly into the operation the hook was ripped right out of Tiffany's arm. Finally, Jeff passed out in pain and shock.

At this point, Bill paused a moment. "I hate it when they pass out. I need to get this off and keep it stretched if I want to preserve it for my collection. But it is no fun at all to do it while they are like this." Again Bill kicked Jeff's head, but this time got no reaction. "Damn," Bill said to himself and completed his removal of Jeff's tattoo. Blood was pouring from Jeff's arm and beginning to pool on the floor under his head.

Bill walked out of the room with his prize. In a few minutes he returned without it. Sitting on the table, he looked at Tiffany and began talking, "Have you ever seen someone totally broken? Completely willing to do anything without question? It is a beautiful thing. Your friend Jeff is weak. I can see that already. But it will be fun for you to observe what I can make him do. Normally I wouldn't waste too much time on him. But for your education I will take my time. You, on the other hand, I think will be a challenge. Oh I have no doubt you are a tramp and that you would do most any disgusting thing to get out of here. But that is simply because you do disgusting things anyway. I believe really breaking you, though, will take some additional imagination."

"You are crazy, you know. Anyone, if tortured enough, will break. You know that. How can you be so impressed with yourself for achieving something that anyone can do?" Tiffany had little confidence that logic would work but she was not about to give up.

"Anyone can paint, anyone can sing. But, there is a difference between an amateur and a real pro. As far as being crazy, have you ever seen a cat catch a mouse? He will play with the mouse first before killing it. No one thinks a cat is crazy. Do you? It is just the way nature is. I am just a product of Mother Nature myself. Maybe I should have been a cat, ideally a tiger. Maybe that is what I'll come back as in my next life. But for now, I just have to be me." Bill smiled and gazed for a moment at Tiffany.

He is totally insane, she thought. She also realized that she and Jeff would likely be dead within a few hours. She had already gotten to the point where she was thinking the sooner the better. Her head and shoulders hurt tremendously. The rip in her arm where the hook had been torn out was still bleeding but the pain from it had subsided. Her underarm had stopped bleeding, but the pain from it combined with the overall pain she had in the shoulder. She thought one or more of her ribs had been broken or something else had been seriously damaged by the blows she had received to her back. Her mind was racing for ideas but none came. The maniac sitting there quietly in front of her was again looking through his tool box. He looked ridiculous, his pudgy, naked body splattered with blood.

"Why us?" asked Tiffany. "What in the world did we ever do to you?"

Bill looked up at her and smiled again. "Fate, I guess," he responded once more in that matter-of-fact tone. "Why does the lion pick a certain zebra over another? It is fate and the opportunity. If you hadn't jumped off the train where you did, you would be halfway to Arizona by now. But fate had other plans for you and for me."

"That is just crap and you know it," Tiffany did not want to give up. "The lion kills for food. You are just doing it for your own evil pleasure. How can you compare yourself with any noble creature? You need help. If you let us down, I promise we won't press charges. We will get you the help you need."

"Very noble of you, I would say. But you have a couple flaws in your logic. First, why do you think I won't be eating both of you later? It saves on the grocery bills and saves a cow or a few chickens." Bill smiled and Tiffany honestly couldn't tell if he was just trying to argue or if he was serious. He was crazy enough to be telling the truth. "Secondly, while I admit that I enjoy what I do, I also think I was put here on earth to cleanse it of those souls whom fate has deemed should no longer be here on earth. Who knows, if I let you live you may have a child that develops a new germ that finds its way out to the general public and starts an epidemic that kills off millions. Perhaps all of mankind. Maybe I am just the scythe of fate sent here to rid the world of its human weeds. I didn't sit by the bridge and wait for you personally to jump off. Fate brought you and not someone else to me. I don't see how you can blame me. It would have been just as easy for fate not to have allowed anyone off the train today. Then none of this would have happened. I believe your friend here is proof of my theory, too. He is really a weak little piece of scum. Within an hour from now I will have him torturing you and wanting to kill you just so I will leave him alone. I could do the same with you, and maybe I will. But first I want you to see me prove myself correct."

"You are crazy, you know," Tiffany said again, halfway to herself. Bill didn't seem to hear her nor was he paying attention to her at the moment. He leaned over and slapped Jeff across the face a few times. Jeff started to regain consciousness.

"There, just a few more minutes. But first let me fix this." To Tiffany's horror he reached out and grabbed the fishing line with the hook dangling free. As routinely as a mechanic might replace loose cable, Bill grabbed a section of Tiffany's arm and drove the hook into it. This time Tiffany was amazed that she didn't even scream out. She just bit down hard and endured it. "That should hold better," Bill remarked and then leaned back down to Jeff.

"Hey buddy, how are you doing?" Jeff just stared at Bill in shock and terror. "Listen, you already ripped a big gash in this young lady here. Look, right here." Bill bent Jeff's face upward with one hand and with the other grabbed Tiffany's arm. "See what you did. I warned you not to thrash around. You should be able to handle pain better than you did. But I am willing to give you a second chance. I told your friend here that you were worthless, but despite all the suffering you put her through she actually tried to defend you. So don't let her down, again."

Bill walked back to the table and pulled out the drill. Standing by the table he turned it on. The sound alone made both Jeff and Tiffany uncontrollably try to move away. The fishing line again tightened and tugged at both hooks. Tiffany grimaced. Bill just smiled and put the drill back in the box. He then pulled out a set of metal bolt cutters and walked over behind Jeff. Jeff started screaming and jerking around. Bill walked back in front of him. "Hey, slow down. Look at what you are doing to your lady friend." He again raised Jeff's face and pointed it toward Tiffany's arm that was bleeding profusely around the hook. The tip of the hook had come through the skin. "Have some guts."

Bill let go and walked back behind Jeff. Tiffany closed her eyes. Jeff's screams were unbearable to listen to but she couldn't cover her ears. Her entire body shook as Jeff reacted violently, again ripping out the hook from Tiffany's arm. Tiffany almost fainted in pain. Jeff was now babbling and spittle was running out of his mouth.

"Look what you did you idiot," shouted Bill, "you hurt your lady friend again." Bill let the loose hook dangle. "Now try to control yourself."

Tiffany looked on in horror as Bill moved back behind Jeff and continued his vicious attack. Jeff recoiled in pain until finally he passed out again. Bill looked down at him and shook his head. He moved back to the table and once more perched himself on it.

As if nothing at all happened, he started talking to Tiffany again. "Do you think that lightning is evil when it strikes and kills a person? Of course not. Is a virus evil when it kills a child? Of course not. Is a soldier evil when he kills his enemy? Is a mother evil when she aborts a baby? Killing is not evil. I don't see what I am doing as evil. It is what fate put me on the earth to do. If it wasn't me, it would be someone else. If it wasn't you, it would be someone else." He smiled again at Tiffany.

"I think this time, though, fate wants you to let us go." Tiffany remarked, saying anything that might stop him. "Let us go and you will see it is what fate has planned for us. I know fate does not want me to die now."

"We'll see. Fate has not steered me wrong yet. I have been doing this for as long as I can remember and I haven't regretted it. I have this house, this land, and now you. Maybe I won't kill you right away. You may be right, it may be better to develop a long term relationship.   But your immediate threat is your friend here. I imagine he is about at the point that he would gladly sacrifice your life for his."

Tiffany didn't answer him. She didn't believe it but at the same time she did not want to challenge him. He didn't need an incentive to be any more wicked than he already was. She also started thinking she did not want to have a long term relationship with this maniac. Bill was crouched down in front of Jeff again trying to bring him back into consciousness. It was taking a while.

As Jeff started showing signs of regaining awareness, Bill stood back up and studied the two of them. Suddenly he walked out of the room, returning in a minute with some rope, an electric cord and an odd looking electrical switch. The switching mechanism was a metal bar that was held in place by a spring. Bill looked at Tiffany and when he saw she was watching him, he lifted the metal bar and released it letting the spring snap it back down into contact with the electrode completing the circuit.

"This is my own little invention, you'll love it." He said with a sick grin. Tiffany doubted that.

He opened the switch again and placed one end of the rope between the metal rod and the electrode. Tiffany noticed that the end of the rope was actually attached to a piece of solid plastic. It was this plastic that Bill had carefully inserted between the metal bar and the electrode. He plugged one end of the cord into an electric socket in the wall and plugged other end of the electrical cord into the bottom of the switch. After he had the switch plugged into the wall, Bill attached another wire to the other side of the switch. Once done he walked back over to Tiffany and to her horror fastened exposed ends of the electric wire to her right thigh with duct tape.

"Oh," Bill murmured, "this will burn and leave one heck of a scar." He grinned and walked back to his tool box. He closed his tool box, picked it up and then set it down right in front of Jeff's face. Bill picked up the free end of the rope and tied it into a knot. Tiffany watched the rope, terrified that his tying the knot may pull the plastic attached at the other end of the rope out from the switch and allow the electrical circuit to close. She could not imagine how horrible being shocked like this might be. Bill then set the knotted end of the rope on top of the closed tool box just inches from Jeff's face.

"Now let's see what kind of a gentleman he is." Tiffany had no idea what Bill was going to do. Tied up the way he was, Jeff did not appear to be able to do anything at all.

Jeff was coming to and Bill leaned close to him and whispered something into Jeff's ear. Tiffany thought he must be explaining the rope resting in front of him and the switch as he pointed to it. Jeff shouted at him, "You are sick, man, sick. If I get out of here I am going to kill you." Bill just leaned back down and whispered something again to Jeff.

"No!" Jeff screamed and again began to thrash around violently. Bill walked back to the tool box and pulled out the drill, turning it on. "No! For god's sake, no!" Jeff screamed again.

Bill moved behind Jeff with the drill still running. Suddenly Jeff arched sharply in pain.

"Do it!" Bill shouted. "Now!"

Jeff howled in pain and rage. Tiffany began praying quietly to herself, something she had not done in years. She was praying as much for Jeff as for herself. She could not imagine the pain he was going through.

Suddenly, Tiffany who had been watching in terror saw Jeff reach out to the rope with his mouth. He seized the knot with his teeth and gave it a hard yank pulling the plastic out from the switching mechanism. The bar snapped shut onto the electrode closing the electric circuit.

Tiffany screamed and tried to pull her leg away from the electrical cord. Instantly she realized, however, that nothing had happened. Jeff had his teeth deep into the rope. He looked up at Tiffany and saw her staring down at him. He started to cry.

Bill had moved back in front of them and leaned down close to Jeff. "You would have sacrificed her for yourself. You are really scum." Without warning Bill rammed the drill bit into Jeff's swollen jugular vein as it pulsed just under his chin. He switched the drill on and it sputtered trying to spin. Within seconds Jeff was dead.

Bill sat back onto the floor as the blood spread around him. His upper torso was rocking slowly, rhythmically back and forth. He looked up at Tiffany with glazed eyes, "Whew, did you see that? That was great."

Tiffany thought he started humming to himself softly as he squatted there rocking slowly with his eyes now shut.

Chapter 17

While I didn't know it until later, I was on my way to the Sheriff's house as Sarah was bathing and Jeff was dying. I had just showered and was preparing to go to bed myself when he called. He wanted to talk and commented that his wife wanted to meet this stranger that he had been talking about so much the last couple of days. A light dinner was the bribe. I would have gone anyway but the light dinner sounded good.

The directions to his house were easy to follow. He lived just outside the city but that was still only a mile or two from city center. Before long I was pulling into a lengthy driveway that led up to a nice looking single story home. Made with brick, the house was on a piece of land that was slightly higher than Denton. The front of the house faced the city lights. The front yard was nicely manicured.

Despite the New Mexico climate, one could do wonders with a yard if they put their mind to it. My yard was a mess. I wondered who took care of their yard, my guess was his wife.

As I pulled in, the front door opened and the Sheriff stepped out. "I appreciate your coming out."

He came down off the porch and shook my hand. "Come on in, Sherry has some excellent snacks set out. She wouldn't let me have any until you arrived."

He looked relaxed. I was happy for that, as I knew the strain was getting to him. Once inside the house we moved through the foyer directly into a large family room or den. The room was decorated with heavy wooden furniture and a western motif. It looked nice and fit the room well, but would not have been something I would have purchased for myself. A number of plates with a wide variety of snacks were scattered about the room. Deviled eggs, finger sandwiches, chips and salsa, small slices of cake, and more were available.

"Are we expecting more guests, Sheriff?" I asked.

"Call me Gene, please," Sheriff Gibbs responded, "and no, no one else is expected. Don't worry we can put a big dent into this." He grinned and picked up a deviled egg.

Just then an attractive woman about the same age as the Sheriff entered through a doorway that I imagined led to the kitchen.

"Hi, I'm Sherry," she introduced herself and came over to shake my hand. "Welcome to our home and to Denton, Mr. West."

"Please call me Jim," I replied. "You have a nice home, Sherry." Close up she was even more attractive. She had a warm smile and a very healthy, outdoor look about her. "Who takes care of the front yard? I bet you do."

"If the yard had to wait on Gene, it would never get done. But he will do quick work on those eggs, Jim. If you want some, you better not hesitate." We both moved over to the coffee table where the eggs were located. I took one. As expected it was delicious. I reached over for one of the finger sandwiches.

"This is my favorite way to eat. Lots of choices and lots of food." Gene agreed with me with a nod.

We stood and then sat in the den for some time eating the

food and talking about the weather, life in Denton, their house, most everything but the ongoing investigation.

On request Sherry brought out some bottled beer. It was a very pleasant evening. They were both good company. When we got to the point where we simply couldn't eat any more, Gene suggested we all move out back and the men have a cigar under the stars. Although I don't smoke, an occasional cigar was okay.

The backyard was as well taken care of as the front. The house had a large concrete patio. The first fifteen or so feet of the patio was covered by the roof but its sides were open. The remaining thirty or so feet of the patio was wide open. A table with a few chairs sat at the far reaches of the concrete. We walked out to the table, getting away from the house lights. It was dark. I could see where the grass stopped, maybe another thirty feet further out and the open fields took over.

"How much land do you own?" I asked them.

"There is a chain link fence about a hundred yards or so out there. It marks our boundary. The fence goes all the way around to the road out front. We just have a handful of acres. Not much. Land here is not expensive." I guess he wanted to make sure I didn't get too impressed with his property.

We sat there under the moonlight and talked about life in general. The phone rang and the Sheriff jumped up and trotted off toward the house.

For a few seconds we sat there in quiet. Then in a somewhat hushed tone, Sherry started talking, "Jim, I certainly appreciate your helping Gene. You can't imagine the internal pressure he puts on himself. He is a very good person and I believe a super

Sheriff. However, he has a terrible time accepting failure. He somehow feels it is his fault that these murders have gone unsolved. As a result, when poor Rick was killed he blamed himself for his death. I know it is absurd. In some ways he knows it, too. But he can't beat back the emotional crisis he is quietly going through inside. It scares me. I know if he can't solve this he will retire from being Sheriff. If someone else, heaven forbid, gets killed I don't know what he will do."

"I knew he was under some stress, but I didn't know the killings had affected him so personally. You know, he doesn't look that bad," I tried to reassure her. "Has he tried counseling? There are hundreds of different counseling programs out there for individuals in law enforcement."

"We have talked about it," Sherry continued, "but he feels it would be a sign of weakness. He doesn't want to undermine the confidence of the people in Denton."

"You know that's silly. First I don't know if seeing a counselor once a week would reflect that badly on him or anyone. Second, he could see one in private and no one would have to know." I had known people, men in particular, like the Sheriff before. They looked at any form of counseling as a weakness and as a quick way to having to compromise their own beliefs. I also knew I was being somewhat hypocritical, as I refused the support of a marriage counselor. A stubborn effort which simply ensured the divorce that I fought so hard against occurring happened anyway.

"Luckily," I took a different tactic, "I think we are getting close to a breakthrough in this case. I have my fingers crossed something will pop within a day or two. I plan on staying here and helping out until it does."

Sherry took my hand and squeezed it. "Thanks," she said.

The door opened and Sheriff Gibbs emerged from the house. "Nothing significant," he informed us, "a truck overturned just outside the city. A lot of debris and traffic problems but fortunately no fatalities. The guys have it well in hand."

We stayed outside and talked for almost another hour. Sherry went back inside shortly after the Sheriff returned to the table. I thought the investigation would pop back up as a topic of conversation, but it never did.

"I noticed that there is no city police organization, just your Sheriff's department. Why is that?" I asked

"Denton actually had one for a while in the sixties, maybe the early seventies, I believe." He answered. "But it cost too much and the police chief was a drunk. I think the city leadership decided that due to the small size of the town and the good work being done by the Sheriff and his crew that the city police department was not really needed. You know that is really not that uncommon. Denton is of the size now that we could probably use a city police department. But, police departments are expensive and the city has been happy with having us do the job for them. For my part, I enjoy the relationship with the city and they do throw some dollars into the department."

"From what I see, you do a good job." I added, not to butter him up, but more so in response to his wife's comments.

Later, we discussed the wildlife that was common around Denton. For some time I listened to his interesting accounts of snakes being found in and around the house. He had never been bitten, but on a number of occasions had close calls with rattlesnakes. He had also had coyotes and other wild animals show up in and around his yard. He and his wife had a pet cat that they worried about due to the wild animals, but their cat seemed to know to stay close to the house.

Before they had put the fence up around the yard, they even had antelope come into their yard at night to eat the flowers and other vegetation.

When we got up to call it a night, I asked him jokingly if it was safe to walk back to the house in the dark. He laughed and said that reminded him of another snake story. One night after cleaning up following a party, his wife was surprised by a large diamondback rattlesnake that had crawled up onto the patio. Fortunately the snake's rattle had given her enough warning for her to avoid the snake.

I asked him what they did with the snake. He replied that whenever possible they put a big trash can over the snake and then call a friend, who would come and take the snake back out to the country to release it. He guessed there had been four or five that they had sent back out in the country. Gibbs said he and his wife often laughed at the possibility that maybe it was just one snake that kept coming back.

As we walked back into the house in the dark, I listened for any noise at all that could foretell the presence of a snake. Silly, I thought, but I still listened apprehensively. I survived the short journey to the house and after saying my thanks soon found myself driving back to the hotel. I thought of going by Sarah's house but decided against it.

It was a pleasant drive and after arriving at the hotel, I turned the television on for a few minutes looking for an old movie. I found an old Bogart movie, Key Largo. I had seen it a few times before and watched it for about a half an hour before I turned it off and went to sleep. I slept well that night.

Chapter 18

Tiffany was doing everything she could to control herself. She knew she was probably going to be killed, but she didn't want to break in front of this maniac. He looked totally insane sitting there as Jeff's blood flowed around him. He seemed to be in some sort of a trance, breathing deeply as though he was trying to absorb all the air around him. His eyes were shut. His arms were relaxed and resting on his thighs. She thought he was murmuring something to himself but if he was it was too soft to be understood. She didn't want to interrupt him. Hopefully, he would stay like this for a long time.

Unfortunately, he did not. After only a few minutes in his trance like position, he looked up and smiled at Tiffany.

"Next," was all he said as he started to get up.

Tiffany tried to look defiant but it was too much to bear. She started crying and then her body collapsed as she finally succumbed to the pain and stress she was suffering. She fainted and hung there by her wrists.

Bill thought about trying to revive her but then had another thought. "Maybe I need to bring you another friend. There has been someone I have been looking for. Don't go anywhere, I'll be back soon." He walked out of the room leaving a trail of bloody footprints behind him. He turned off the overhead light. Tiffany hung there quietly in the dark.

Outside, it was also dark. Bill was surprised to see how late it was.   He figured Sarah Stone was in her house by now. Probably sleeping he thought.   He went and showered.   He watched as the blood on his body washed down the drain.   He would have left it on longer as he actually enjoyed being covered with his victim's blood.   But he knew he couldn't be outside driving around with the blood on him.

After the shower, Bill came up with his plan.   Rather than going to her house now and breaking in, he would sleep for a short while and then go by her house just before dawn.   He set his alarm and climbed into his bed.   For the next few hours, Bill slept as peacefully as a baby.   It had been a good day.

Downstairs, Tiffany had come out of her faint and was desperately trying to free herself from her chains.   It was dark and quiet and while she was unaware how long she had been out, she was certain she was alone and this might be her last chance.   She struggled feverishly only semi-aware that her wrists were now bleeding freely where the chains had worn them raw.

Bill jumped out of bed at the sound of his alarm clock.   He quickly got dressed and out to his car, carefully locking his front door behind him.   Burglaries were rare around Denton but better safe than sorry.   He had twice been a victim of a breaking and entering in Washington D. C..   For a long time he tried to come up with ways to catch a burglar, any burglar, so he could take his revenge.   He never succeeded.

Bill drove straight to Sarah's street and parked down the road from her house.   The street was dark as were all the houses.   It was just after five in the morning.   He debated whether he should just break in and grab her or if he should wait for a while to see if she might come outside while the rest of the street was still quiet.

The odds were a lot better if he just went in and got her. He was about to do just that when two things happened that made him change his mind. First, a car went by with someone throwing the morning paper into subscribers' yards. One of the yards was Sarah's. Then, almost in synch with the arrival of the paper, a light went on in Sarah's house. Then a second light was turned on.

Bill decided to move his car down closer. There were a few other cars parked on the street so he didn't think one more would draw anyone's attention. A light came on further down the street. He would have to be careful and do something soon. He got out of his car and darted into Sarah's yard. He hid by some large shrubbery that lined part of the house. Looking around he saw that the neighborhood was still quiet. He was not used to operating in a residential neighborhood and he found his anxiety thrilling. Maybe he would do more of this in the future. He had heard of tigers going right into villages at night and stealing away with their victims. In his demented mind, Bill tried to envision himself as a tiger among its sleeping prey.

He was surprised when he heard Sarah's door open. He leaned back further against the wall of the house. Sarah stepped out of the house in a jogging outfit. She closed the door behind her and walked straight out to the morning paper. She was just going to throw it off the wet grass back onto the porch until she returned. It was her routine to jog a couple of miles each morning and return home to read the morning paper in its entirety each day before going to work. Reading the paper was something that she had been encouraged to do since her first day at the job. It required her waking up a little earlier than usual but she felt it was her responsibility as a key member of the staff employed by the newspaper.

Bill watched her walk out into the yard not far from him. He quickly realized what she was going to do. Perfect, he thought. As she leaned over to pick up the paper he jumped out at her, catching her completely by surprise. She made a muffled scream as he leapt onto her back. Before she could get out another sound Bill hit her hard on her exposed right temple with his fist and she blacked out. Bill had brought with him a pistol, a knife and a small, heavy metal baton. In the end, all he needed was his fist. He was pleased with his work. He quickly picked Sarah up and carried her to his truck. He threw her into the passenger seat and ran around to the driver's side. Jumping in, he started the truck and drove off. A quick glance around let him see that no more lights had gone on and more than likely no one noticed the event that just took place in their neighborhood. Yes, Bill thought, he may want to try more of this in the future. What a rush.

Bill, worried that Sarah would regain her consciousness before he got her home, pulled off behind the old closed gas station on the outskirts of town and quickly bound her hands behind her with duct tape and then sealed her mouth shut with more tape. He made sure her nose was uncovered. He didn't want her to die, just yet.

He had only driven a short distance when Sarah started regaining consciousness. Suddenly she started thrashing about trying to get her hands free. When she realized where she was, she started to raise her legs to kick at Bill. He simply drew out his gun and pointed it at her.

"Whichever leg kicks me first, gets shot first. Your call, lady. Sit tight. I just want to know what you know." Bill was hoping to have her stay still.

Bill would not have minded shooting her, but he certainly did not want to get blood in his truck. He knew from a lot of experience that blood was hard to clean out of car upholstery. She stopped moving and sat looking at him.

Sarah's mind was now racing. She knew immediately who this was. It had to be Bill White. He was about the right age and appearance, if you could rely on those old high school yearbooks. She was furious with herself for letting him surprise her so. She never considered herself helpless, but she had sure let herself get into a position that was starting to look that way. She wondered what he wanted with her. She would have thought he would have just killed her when he had the chance. The fact that he didn't gave her some hope. But only because Sarah didn't realize that a quick death was not something that Bill White ever wanted to give to one of his victims. If she had known the truth she would have been utterly terrified.

Sarah tried playing with the door handle behind her as she sat facing Bill. There was a possibility if she could open the door that she could throw herself out and, if she survived the fall out of the car, start running across open country to get away. The door handle moved but the door didn't open. Bill had either done something to the door or the pickup had a version of a child safety lock.

In a few minutes they pulled into a driveway and drove up to a rundown looking house. Dawn was just starting to break but it was still fairly dark. Sarah looked around and didn't see another house or any cars on the lonely stretch of road that ran in front of the house. She knew she would have just a second or two to make her move.

Bill wasn't cooperating. After he stopped the car, he climbed out and walked around to her side. He drew his pistol again and moved back away from the car as soon as he opened the door. Sarah was going to use that opportunity to make her move, kicking him as hard as she could and then running. But he was too far away.

"Walk, toward the house. Don't do anything silly or I will shoot your knees out." Bill cautioned. Sarah had no doubt that he was telling the truth. She got to the door and stopped. With her hands tied behind her she could not open the door. She looked back at Bill and stepped away from the door. He moved up and reached for the door knob. As he did so Sarah saw her opportunity. She kicked out at Bill hitting him solid on his left hip. The kick hurt Bill and knocked him momentarily off balance.

Sarah spun around and started to run. She had only gone about ten yards when the shot rang out and a searing pain went through her left leg. The bullet had just grazed her, but she stopped in her tracks. She was too close and he could easily get several more shots off before she could get far enough away to be safe. She slowly turned around to face her antagonist. She only got partially turned around before she was hit again upside her head. This time it wasn't just a fist. Bill hit her with the pistol and as she was staggering, hit her again. She collapsed to the ground. Bill had to summon most of his will power to not continue striking her. Finally, he leaned over and dragged her into his house.

Tiffany had already given up on trying to work herself free. She could no longer feel her hands. Her head and shoulders throbbed. She was convinced something was broken inside her and her whole body hurt every time she moved. All she could do was hang there and wish that either someone would come save her or that her captor would let her die a quick death. She knew both were long shots.

The door opened behind her. Tiffany tensed. She hoped beyond hope that it was not her tormentor.

"Hey, I have brought you a friend." Terrified, Tiffany knew her hopes were over. She didn't even try to turn around. The light came back on and Tiffany had to close her eyes. She heard Bill chuckle at her discomfort. He was next to her and was touching, no rubbing her stomach gently. Then he stopped. Tiffany opened her eyes and tried to let them adjust to the light. Bill had moved away from her and was unhooking Jeff from the ceiling. Jeff collapsed onto the floor and was roughly dragged to the corner of the room right in front of them. Then Bill moved back behind her and she heard the sound of clothing being ripped or cut.

Moments later he was back next to her, struggling to hang a limp female up on the same chains that moments earlier had held Jeff. It looked awkward but within a minute or two the other female was hanging next to Tiffany. She was bleeding from the leg and from a gash on the side of her head.

Her captor moved back in front of her. "Look at you two. You both could be Playboy models. In fact I am going to get my camera. My friends will be most envious." He walked out of the room.

Tiffany looked over at her fellow prisoner. She was older than Tiffany, maybe by ten years. Hanging there, bruised and bleeding, Tiffany could still tell that she was pretty and had the build of an athlete or at least someone who stayed in excellent shape. Tiffany noticed there was no wedding band on her left hand. Silly, Tiffany thought, to notice such an irrelevant thing at this time.

Tiffany thought that Bill must not use his camera very often as he was taking a long time in returning. That was just fine with her. With any luck he was still using the old fashioned cameras and would have to go to the store and get some film. She thought she must be losing her own mind as she almost started giggling at her predicament. Feeling light headed she wondered how much blood a person had to lose before she died. Maybe she was getting close to that point. There was a lot of blood on the floor below her but nothing in comparison with the blood that came out of Jeff. Poor Jeff, she thought. She would have liked to have been able to console his mom when she found out about his death. Jeff's mother was a sweet lady who would now be alone. Poor old lady.

All of a sudden Bill was next to her again. He went in and out of focus. Tiffany thought she was starting to pass out again. Hopefully this time it would be for good. She heard someone shouting close by and snapped out of her trance. The person hanging next to her had regained consciousness and was shouting at the man that was holding them both captive. He was just sitting there on the table smug and smiling. Tiffany had not registered in her mind what all was screamed at their tormentor but she got the impression the lady hanging next to her knew the madman in front of them. That impression was quickly confirmed.

"You know, Ms. Stone," their captive calmly stated, "I am impressed that you know who I am. It seems my stay in this town will have to come to an end. I am curious to know a few things first. One, how did you figure out who I was? Two, did that other reporter tell you or anyone else about me? And, three, who have you told? Obviously not the police as they have not bothered me at all."

"I am not the only one who knows you are a murderer. Everyone else does by now. I imagine even the North Carolina police are on their way right now." Sarah responded defiantly. "Your only chance is to turn yourself in." She knew she was bluffing but she wanted to somehow affect the upper hand he had in dealing with her. Something she said did get to him. She saw it immediately in his eyes.

"Then why haven't the police come to get me?"

Despite his rebuttal, Bill was stunned. The reference to North Carolina went back years to crimes that he had even started to forget. How could she possibly know about North Carolina? What all did she know? How dangerous was his situation right now? Without explanation, he stood up and left the room closing the door behind him but leaving the light on.

Bill went upstairs and automatically started packing his things. He would transfer the money later that day to another bank, maybe to a bank out of the country. He had heard that there were Mexican banks in which one could hide money from the U.S. authorities. He could drive to Mexico in six maybe seven hours he thought. He went and found an old road map and started studying routes to the south.

Why haven't they come for him, he pondered the question again. Then it came to him. They may have figured out who was responsible for the killings but they did not know where he was. It was obvious. The authorities were looking for Bill White, a man in his late thirties. Not the old man everyone thought lived in this house, a man in his late sixties. Only one person in town had actually seen through the disguise and she was now dead.

Bill sat back down and took a deep breath. He would still have to leave and sooner rather than later. But there was no emergency. He figured he had another day or so. He went into his dirty little kitchen and made some hot chocolate for himself. His mind was still in a whirl. Maybe he should just kill the two women in the basement quickly and move on to preparing his escape. But he had wanted so much to completely dominate and destroy the one with the eyes. She had the type of eyes that seemed to penetrate you and Bill had always been fascinated with the few people he had seen with eyes like that. She had been hurt considerably already but she was nowhere near breaking. He loved her type. He had only run into a few before, mostly female. He wondered why that was. Somewhere he thought he had read that women handle pain better than men. Maybe so, he thought.

He buttered some bread and ate it. Bread and hot chocolate

were his routine breakfast.

He had no real interest in the other woman, Sarah Stone. Killing her quickly might be necessary, not his preferred way of doing things but it would allow him to get out of town quicker. More importantly, he wanted to drive the younger one to the point where she would kill Stone for him. Then he could laugh right in her face while he killed her. Bill started to calm down. He thought he could have the whole thing accomplished before noon. He could then pack and get organized. Hell, he could even leave after dark that same day if everything went as he planned.

It was already daylight outside. He had better get started, there was little time left. Tossing the remaining hot chocolate into the dirty sink, Bill went to the stairs and down to the basement.

Chapter 19

The next morning, I was up and shaving when the phone rang. I thought to myself that at least Sarah let me sleep in a little this morning. When I answered the phone however, it wasn't Sarah.

"Jim, we got some interesting news from Marge this morning. Can you get in here right away?" It was the Sheriff. "And, if you don't mind my asking is Sarah there with you?"

"No, I haven't seen her since before coming out to your place. Why do you ask?" My apprehension was already building.

"It may not be anything. I don't mean to worry you, it's just we have been trying to get in touch with her this morning and as of right now no one has been able to find her. We have a couple of deputies going by the house right now. Come on in to the office and we can go over what we have."

My mind was racing. "Okay, I'll be there in a few minutes. Let me get dressed and shaved." I added. I was already on my way out the door but I needed the few extra minutes.

Outside I jumped into my car and drove straight to Sarah's house. It was only a few minutes away. When I arrived the deputies were already there. They were both leaning against their vehicle which was parked in her driveway. Sarah's car was still in the driveway. The house looked peaceful.

"What's up?" I was almost shouting and tried to calm myself down. "Is Sarah inside?"

"If she is she is not answering the door or the phone. The house is locked up. We are awaiting the go ahead to go in. We should get it soon," responded one of the two.

The other did not appear as friendly. "We would prefer if you went and waited somewhere else. If you check with the Sheriff later he will probably let you know what we find. We don't need any civilians disturbing the scene."

I counted to ten before I responded. Despite my strong feelings, I knew I didn't hold the upper hand in this argument. "I'm going to see the Sheriff right now anyway. He wanted to discuss something with me." Turning, I walked to my car. As there was no sign of a break-in at the house and it was still locked, my guess was that Sarah was not there. Unfortunately, whether she was or wasn't didn't make much difference right now. Until someone located her and I found out she was okay, my fears and anxiety weren't going to subside.

I was at the Sheriff's office within five minutes and was ushered right into his office. "I hear you swung by Sarah's before you came here. I don't blame you, but I am glad you didn't raise a stink with my guys. Have a seat while I get us both some coffee. I definitely need another cup."

He stepped out into the hallway. I sat down but stood back up. I didn't feel like relaxing. My mind was racing. Although I knew I was getting ahead of myself, I started theorizing the possibilities behind Sarah's disappearance. If she was kidnapped by the same person who had killed the others, it would make sense that the person was local and knew the relationship between Rick and Sarah. It would also mean the killer was still in town or close by. I didn't want to consider the possibility that Sarah could have been murdered. It simply wasn't an option as far as I was concerned. I hadn't got much further in my thinking when the Sheriff walked back in with two large mugs of coffee. I thanked him and sat back down.

I could see right away he was not taking this any better than I was. His eyes looked tired. Actually, I thought, his whole face had a haggard appearance. He looked like life had finally beaten him. When he spoke though, it was hard to discern anything and I quickly began wondering if his wife's comments to me the night before had led me to start seeing things that were not there.

"Marge was able to come up with another piece of the puzzle. Last night she was asking around to see if any of her lady friends could remember Bill White. By chance one of them did. Her son was one of Bill's best friends. She told Marge that Bill had a high school crush on Annie Shell. Despite the difference in ages, Bill White apparently knew and may have had some kind of relationship with Annie. In my mind that makes one too many coincidences. White has to be our guy. Now we just need to find him. Unfortunately, her friend's son has not seen him, or heard from him, since high school."

Wanting to be convinced that we may be on the right track, I nodded. "I agree, I would also suggest you contact the FBI and North Carolina. Tell them you have very good reason to believe that White is still alive and is here. They may be able to help us, although I doubt if that help will come as quickly as we need it. I wish we would hear from Sarah."

"I know. My deputies should be calling me shortly. If she is not in her home, it may mean we have a very small window of time to find her. This guy has not given me any reason to believe that he will let her live for long. God, I hope we are just way ahead of ourselves and she has simply gone somewhere and forgot to tell anyone."

"What made you start looking for her in the first place?" I asked.

"Marge called her at home this morning early and she was not there. She tried the office and she wasn't there either. She tried her cell phone and when that went unanswered she really got worried and called me. I immediately began our look for her. I was hoping she was with you." He gave me a partial smile of support. "We kept coming up with nothing."

Just then one of the uniformed ladies that worked out in front walked in and said to the Sheriff that Sarah was not at the house. There was no sign of a struggle or any sign that would indicate anything out of the ordinary.

"Well, I guess that is about as good as news as possible at this point. Let's hope she turns up soon. We need to find her. I have already obtained the help of the State Highway Patrol. They have her picture and have assigned about a dozen extra officers to work this area. The Highway Patrol will cover the interstate rest areas and larger gas stations along with a couple other state highways. I will contact the FBI and North Carolina. But I don't think we have days to solve this. My guess is that we have a handful of hours at the most."

I told him that I agreed. We had to find her soon.

Sheriff Gibbs continued. "I am going to be sending everyone but the dispatchers out on the streets this morning. The dispatchers will have to pull double duty answering the phones here at the station. You can come along with me or look around yourself if you want."

Interestingly, I got the impression from the Sheriff that he wanted me to operate alone. It made perfect sense, if I went with him I would not be an extra set of eyes and ears. I would just be tagging along. However, I rarely ran into a local Sheriff or Police Chief that encouraged me to go my own way.

"I guess I wouldn't be able to add much if I just followed you around all morning. I'll stay in touch and let you know what I develop." I got up and we both walked to the front door of the station.

"Good luck," the Sheriff added.

"You, too," I figured we all needed it.

I drove back to the hotel. I didn't know the town well enough to start somewhere else. I figured I would talk to the people at the hotel, then the restaurants. Hopefully they would give me some additional leads. There was a possibility my efforts would overlap the Sheriff's folks, but I didn't know what else to do.

The hotel proved negative. Everyone was willing to help and I knew I started the town rumor mill when I began asking questions about Sarah. No doubt the deputies' questions elsewhere were doing the same. On the good side, the rumor may get to someone before we did and that person might call in with info. On the downside, if it got to White, he would likely dispose of any evidence he had and that could include Sarah if he had her.

I next went to the Pancake House. The waitresses there immediately reacted to my questioning. A number of the restaurant's employees quickly surrounded me and started asking questions of their own. Many of them were Sarah's age and had known her for a while. They had a lot of ideas and I began writing them down. There was an aunt she used to visit in Santa Fe, a college friend in Las Vegas, New Mexico, and a ranch south of town where she was friends with a family. The ranch belonged to the Johnson's and was not far from town. It was where she practiced her barrel racing when she was younger.

I used a phone at the restaurant and passed on all the leads to the Sheriff. He was already aware of the aunt. That lead had been checked out without success. He would have to try to reach the other two by phone.

The waitress wanted to know if there had been a struggle or if anyone had seen her kidnapper. I reassured all of them that at this point that there was no sign of a struggle and that we didn't even know if she had been kidnapped. We just wanted to get an early jump on what might prove to be a bad situation, if we couldn't find her safe somewhere. I knew I did not sound too convincing. I found myself already starting to believe the worst had occurred.

I left the restaurant not too sure where to go. I decided to go by the old man's garage where I had the tires replaced on my car. I didn't expect much but it was at least something to do.

I had already started thinking that if we found Sarah alive I wanted to take her to Europe, Asia, anywhere to see the world. I wanted to spend more time with her and to make her happy. She was too young to die.

I made a wrong turn in the city and got frustrated. I pulled into the parking lot of a hardware store to make a u-turn and to try to get back to a point in the city where I could get my bearings. As I did, I observed Dave Hepp and Saul Church emerge from the store carrying a couple of bags.

"Hey, guys," I shouted at them through the window. They stopped and I maneuvered my car next to theirs. "Do you know who Sarah Stone is?"

"Sure," they said in unison.

"She is a babe, everyone knows who she is," added Saul.

"What's up?" asked Dave.

"Maybe nothing, but no one can find her and with all the things going on in town I am trying to locate her." I tried to sound calm but I knew there was an edge to my voice, they probably could sense it.

"I haven't seen her lately," Saul looked at Dave.

"Me neither," added Dave. "Do you think she might be connected with the killings? Surely she couldn't have killed all those people."

"No, our worry is not that she committed the killings, we just hope she hasn't become the latest victim."

"Dummy," Saul said under his breath to Dave.

"As I said, hopefully I am just overreacting. Maybe she just ran off with some young guy like one of you two." I tried to lighten the conversation.

"I wish," they both said in unison.

"If either of you see her, could you call the Sheriff. He is also looking for her. Another thing, did either of you ever know a guy by the name of Bill White? He would probably be in his late thirties now."

"Not me," said Saul.

Dave just shook his head.

"Didn't think you would, just a long shot." I stated.

"Think he is involved?" asked Dave.

"It seems likely but we won't really know until we get this matter solved."

"Is he from Denton? I don't recognize the name." Saul asked, taking his turn.

An interesting couple of guys I couldn't help but think.

"He grew up here and then left to join the Marines. I think he may have come back to Denton." I didn't want to offer too much.

"Are you some kind of secret agent or something?" Dave asked.

I told him I wasn't and repeated my request that they contact the Sheriff if they saw Sarah or heard anything at all that might lead us to her whereabouts.

They both acknowledged that they would.

I thanked them and drove back to the center of town to regain my bearings. I was starting to feel like our efforts would be in vain. That if we did find her, it would just be after she was dead. Thinking like that did no good at all. I realized that, but I couldn't fight the worry back. It was developing a momentum all to itself.

I wasn't paying attention to where I was going and someone honked at me from behind. I angrily told myself to snap out of it and turned right onto the highway that ran through the town. The horn from a vehicle behind me sounded again. I looked in my rear view mirror and saw a pickup with two men waving at me. It was Dave and Saul. I pulled over to the shoulder of the highway.

They pulled in behind me and we all got out of our vehicles.

"Hey, mister," it was Saul doing the talking. "We just thought of something. While we don't know this White character, there is a stranger we have seen a few times that seems to come and visit the old man that lives out north of here. The old man is kind of a recluse. This younger man could be your guy."

"We think he's gay," added Dave.

I asked for and got directions to the old man's house. They did not know his name but gave me very good instructions. I wondered if the old man happened to be Bill's Dad. I didn't give much credence or interest to the gay allegation.

"Listen, guys, I am going out there right now. It is extremely important that you get this information to the Sheriff right away. It is critical that you do so. Tell him I am headed out that way and will meet him there. Will you do it?" I had already started backing up the car.

They nodded that they would. I had no doubt they would fulfill their mission as effectively as two Eagle Scouts.

I drove fast. If a cop pulled behind me, so much the better I thought. None did. I left the city limits in minutes and it wasn't long after that when I thought I saw the house the boys were referring to. It sat a couple hundred yards off one of the small rural routes that spread out from Denton before just dying at some field or unpaved cross-road. I slowed down as I passed the house and realized immediately that I wasn't far from the spot where I had discovered Rick's body. There was a black pickup truck parked by the house. There were no other signs of life. I drove on by until I cleared a small rise in the road and stopped the car at the bottom of the decline on the other side. I couldn't see the house. I did a u-turn and parked the car just off the road. I got out of the car and walked about ten steps, until I could once again see the house.

There was no movement anywhere. I stood still and watched. As I stood there I realized there was actually a large herd of cattle further off to the north. Additionally, I discovered a small family of antelope not too far from my own position. I marveled how life seemed so peaceful here in the open. Deja-vu, I thought. I had experienced this feeling so many times before. It was like the world and life itself was schizophrenic. Peace and tranquility was often just skin deep. Like many people I thought. Scratch past the surface and killing and suffering abounded.

I knew this lead was just a long shot, but it was all I had at the moment. Certainly the man Saul and Dave had referred to wouldn't be the only occasional visitor to the Denton area. But the scenario and location fit our theories. It was definitely worth checking out.

I saw a car in the distance coming my way from the city. Thinking it was the Sheriff I jumped back into my car and headed towards the house. I should have known better. It would have been very fast for the Sheriff to have already gotten the word and driven here. As I approached the house, the car shot past. It was just a young couple. Instinctively, I pulled into the driveway. Hell, I thought, the Sheriff should be here in just a few minutes. I could easily stall whoever was in the house from going anywhere or, more importantly, doing anything that my mind did not want to think of for at least five minutes.

Chapter 20

As soon as Bill left the basement, Sarah turned and looked at Tiffany. She couldn't believe her eyes. The poor girl had been terribly brutalized. She was covered in blood and looked as though she was close to death. Despite all that had happened to her, Sarah could tell she was a very attractive girl. She was also no one whom Sarah had seen in Denton before. "Who are you?" Sarah asked as she unsuccessfully tried to get her hands and wrists free. "How did you get here?"

"My name is Tiffany. Jeff and I were sneaking rides on trains trying to get to California." Upon saying Jeff's name, Tiffany glanced over at the limp body thrown in the corner. Sarah looked at the body, too. She had already observed it, but now that the body had a name, the horror of her situation just sunk in deeper.

"What did he do to him?" The body looked terribly abused.

"He tortured him for a long time. Then he killed him. This guy is sick. He is really sick. If we don't get out of here he will do the same to us."

"What all has he done to you?" Sarah asked.

Somehow, Tiffany knew what Sarah was really asking. Her cuts and wounds were obvious. Tiffany understood Sarah's question. "He has not raped me, if that is what you are asking. I even tried to bribe him with sex but it didn't work. I do not believe that this guy is into sex. He is into pain and death. He really, really is. He just sat there in Jeff's blood chanting to himself after he finally killed him."

Sarah's fear was getting out of control. Hanging there helpless in some maniac's basement she knew that unless someone could figure out where Bill White was living and get there soon, she was likely going to suffer the same horror as Jeff and the poor girl next to her.

Something the girl had said though brought a thought into Sarah's mind. She regained control over her panic. She had read or seen somewhere in an Associated Press release, or maybe in the Santa Fe newspaper, something about hitch hikers and people illegally riding on trains disappearing. The article went on to say that the FBI had a large dragnet out trying to find who was responsible. She thought something about that had come up yesterday in Jim's phone conversation too.

"You say you were riding on a train?"

"Not legally," admitted Tiffany. "Jeff and I were on one that was just carrying cargo, I guess, no people. We jumped on in Oklahoma City and jumped off where the trains have to slow down for the old bridge just outside of this town. It was raining and when we ran to an old gas station for cover we ran into him." Tiffany motioned her head to infer the maniac upstairs. "He was waiting for us. No, he was waiting for anyone who might get off the train there. I am sure he has done this before."

"I think you're right," said Sarah. "His name is Bill White. I believe he is responsible for a number of murders. No doubt we will be two more of his victims unless we can figure something out or someone comes and rescues us."

"No one will be coming to rescue me. No one knows I am

here. I doubt if anyone even knows that I am even in the state of New Mexico." Tiffany remarked listlessly.

"But they will for me. They won't know where, but they will have a good guess as to the who and the why. My bet is that there is a large search going on right now. Let's try to stall this guy and keep our fingers crossed," Sarah suggested. She knew she sounded more positive than she really felt inside.

"With luck, you will have some time. But not me. I do not know how much longer I have, even if he never comes back. I think I have lost a lot of blood. I get faint now all the time. Plus, I believe he has his mind set on breaking me the way he broke Jeff. I will hold out as long as I can, but no guarantees." Tiffany was staring at Jeff while she talked.

"Hang in there." A stupid remark, Sarah realized at once, as she had no choice while those chains cut into her wrists. "Don't give up yet." Sarah marveled at this young girl. She had been through hell and yet still had some fight left in her. Sarah did not think she could be so resilient. Another thought came to her. "Does he ever let you down, like to go to the bathroom?"

"No, you just go when you need to. I don't think he minds the mess on the floor." Tiffany almost started giggling again but fought the urge off. She knew there was nothing funny about their predicament but she was slowly losing control of her mind.

Sarah studied the room. It was a mess. There was blood all over the floor and splatters on the side of the table in front of them. There were also bloody prints on the table top and on what looked like a tool box on the table. She realized that the flooring was such that it could be mopped clean. Some type of vinyl over concrete she thought. The chains were attached firmly to the ceiling and behind her there looked to be some type of hoist. Maybe to help White with his heavier victims she thought.

"Did anyone else get off the train with you?" Sarah asked. Her instinct as a reporter made her curious despite the situation she was in.

"No, no one even knew we were on the train." Tiffany responded.

As Sarah kept working to get free she asked Tiffany how she knew where to get off and where White was laying in wait for them. Tiffany very briefly told Sarah how they had been told about the bridge, and then explained how White had been parked near the tracks and how he had drugged them.

"You know," she said, then paused. "He gets nude before he starts cutting on us. He looks stupid. Squatty, ugly body." Tiffany's eyes were starting to glaze over again. Sarah thought about trying to talk her back into consciousness but decided not to. The poor girl had been through too much.

The room was quiet. Sarah wondered if Bill had left the house. She was hoping he had. The longer he left her alone, the better. Someone had to have realized by now that she was missing. She knew a search would be underway.

She heard the door squeak behind her. "How are my two young ladies doing?" asked Bill.

"Not good," Sarah responded, "Tiffany needs a doctor. Why don't you make a run for it and leave us here. Just call an ambulance on your way out."

"Tiffany, is that her name? I think that is a pretty name." Bill stood there looking at Tiffany's limp body. "Oh, I think I do need to leave soon, but I can't just run out and leave you here. You are right, she does need a doctor. Did you ever play Doctor and patient when you were a child? I never did but I always wanted to. I think I can be her doctor. I can probably find out what is ailing her, if I dig deep enough."

Sarah thought he was sick enough to do just that.

Bill moved over to his tool box and started looking for something. He looked disappointed. "I hate it when I misplace my tools, don't you?" He came back and sat on the table facing Sarah. "Let's talk for a while until she comes back out of it. I need her awake so she won't miss the grand finale."

"What do you want to talk about?" Sarah was willing to talk about anything if it would just keep him from hurting them for a while longer.

"How much do you know about me?" Bill asked.

"We know a lot about you, although I admit most of it just came to us in the past two days." Sarah responded accentuating the "we".

It worked. "Who is the we?" Bill demanded.

"The sheriff and all his people. The state police, the FBI, the authorities in North Carolina, and of course, my newspaper." She paused for a while to let it sink in. "Let me ask you one question. Why did you kidnap me?"

"You were that other reporter's lover. He stumbled onto me. Well not exactly, but close enough. I thought he may have shared his theory with you. Had he?" Bill asked.

"No, I do not have any idea about any theory he may have had. Besides I was not his lover."

Bill was starting to wonder how much else he had gotten wrong. He thought this lady was telling him the truth. If his logic was off, he may be in more danger than he thought. The mention again of the North Carolina authorities and now the FBI did startle him. His paranoia was increasing.

"What all do you know about me?" He asked.

Sarah decided to try a long shot. "First, we know about the hitch hikers and transients on the trains." She stared at him when she said this and saw a reaction. It was true, she thought. This was the person responsible for the missing people. "Where do you bury them all?"

Bill didn't even hear her last question. The blood was rushing to his mind. He was feeling light headed. How could they know about his killings? No one should have known. He had seen nothing in the press, although he rarely watched the news or read the newspaper. He had heard nothing, but this young reporter in this little hick town had known. That meant others must know.

"Where do you bury them?" Sarah repeated.

"All over," Bill murmured. He seemed lost in thought. Then he looked up at Sarah. She could see the emotions in his face were turning into anger and hate. She realized that she may have pushed a wrong button.

He stood up and came at her. She started to say something but she was surprised at his speed and strength in punching her in the stomach. He struck three hard blows. The first one took the wind out of her and the next two crashed against her ribs.

She started to sob. She didn't want to but her loss of breath and sudden additional pain just overwhelmed her.

"How do you know all this?" Bill shouted. He felt his secure world starting to collapse.

"Listen," he shouted, slapping Sarah's face, "you can either die quickly or slowly. Your choice, but you need to tell me how much everyone knows." Bill had already decided he would have to kill them both quickly, as he had to make good his escape as soon as possible.

"I don't know how much the FBI knows." Sarah bluffed. "The Sheriff knows you are in town, or nearby. I know he has help coming from the state and the FBI. They will be dropping a dragnet around this part of the state. They have probably already started. Your kidnapping me will only motivate them even more. Let us go and I will testify on your behalf. You just need help. You don't need to go to jail."

"They will never capture me alive, don't you worry about that. How did they figure out I was grabbing the hitch hikers?" Bill never left a witness. He thought he had never left the police any clues. The hitchhikers were easy prey. Pick them up along the highway, drug them, and then bring them here to his basement. "You still haven't told me. There is no way they could have known."

"I don't know. The FBI's has the lead in investigating the missing hitch hikers, not the Sheriff. I just know the last I heard they had you targeted as the prime suspect and were sending a team here to help the Sheriff locate you." Sarah was making it up as she went along.

Tiffany jerked next to them. Still unconscious, some of her muscles were starting to spasm.

"Look at her dance," remarked Bill. He moved over to

Tiffany and grabbed her face with his right hand. He shook her whole head. "Hey, Sweetie, time to wake up."

Tiffany's eyes opened. They didn't look as though they were focusing though.

"Time to get on with our business," Bill said with a smile. Sarah realized that he was about to do something horrible.

Bill backed up to the table and pulled his sweatshirt and t-shirt off. He folded them on the far corner of the table. "Mustn't get the clothes all dirty," he said with a smile to Sarah. "I hate to do laundry, don't you?" His question was so detached and matter-of-fact like that Sarah thought that he was actually just making normal conversation. Despite this insane situation and the bizarre environment they were in, here in the basement, Bill could calmly talk about doing laundry. Sarah knew at that point that there was no way out. Unless someone came fast to rescue them they would both be dead in the next few minutes.

Chapter 21

On his part, the Sheriff had gotten a call from the office that two young men were there to see him saying it was very important. He quickly returned to the office and debriefed Dave and Saul. It was a long shot, but at least it was a lead they could pursue with some hope. The sheriff thanked the two and grabbed Deputy Beverly Richardson who had been with him that morning interviewing Sarah's friends and neighbors.

Sheriff Gibbs departed the Sheriff's station with Deputy Richardson determined to set the new land speed record from his office to the house. A person who may be White had been seen at the residence a couple of times. That was all he needed to throw caution to the wind.

The Sheriff was trying to recall the old man who lived there. He may have seen him a few times, but he couldn't recall who he was. They were soon approaching the house.

"Damn," he said to Deputy Richardson. "West must already be in the house. I wish he would have waited. We don't even know if White is here or what name he may go by now. The old man may not know him as Bill White."

Deputy Beverly Richardson's adrenaline was really spiking. The Sheriff's high speed driving hadn't helped, but it was only a contributing factor. The truth was that this was the first physical pursuit of a dangerous killer that Beverly Richardson had ever been on. Furthermore, she fully realized that if their lead was accurate, she and the Sheriff could well be the first to make contact with the killer. She did not know how far behind backup was, but it was obvious that the Sheriff was not going to be waiting for it. In fact, she wasn't sure if he had even asked for back-up.

Beverly had only been with the Sheriff's department for two years. She had mostly been assigned duties with juvenile crime and with special events. She had seen action in helping other deputies break up fights but that was about the height of her confrontations with danger. She had joined the Sheriff's Department after a year at college had proved too expensive for her family and emotionally a strain on her. Always a fairly conservative individual, Beverly found that most of her classmate's at the large public university were more interested in booze and sex than in getting a college degree. She tried at first not to join in but the peer pressure became too great. A large mistake as she was unable to handle the alcohol and the emotional strain that came with her new life as a "party girl." She vowed to herself when she finally left college that never again would she so compromise her principles. She worked briefly at a department store in town and after reading an ad in the local paper, made her move into law enforcement. She was happy with her job. The pay was not great but it covered her bills and she liked the people with whom she worked.

It wasn't that she was now afraid. Things were moving too fast for that. It was just that she had always wondered how she would do in a truly tough situation. She had heard about other deputies who froze at the critical moment and had either failed to make an arrest, or worse, had been killed. Faced with a deadly confrontation, could she pull the trigger? She thought she could. But, could her hand stay still enough to hit what she was aiming at? She wasn't too sure about that.

Beverly had total confidence in the Sheriff. For that matter, like so many of the young women who worked at the department, she had a crush on him. His bearing and professionalism along with his warm personality made him a natural target for the affection and daydreams of many of the females that worked with him. Beverly doubted he ever noticed.

She was extremely pleased that morning when the Sheriff divided the entire department up into teams and he selected her to be his partner. He had tried to place a female with every male as he thought it might help in the search for Sarah Stone. There were not enough female deputies to go around, but she was fortunate to end up with Sheriff Gibbs.

Beverly was not fully cognizant of all the facts in the case but knew enough to understand the man they were pursuing was believed to have been responsible for all the recent killings in Denton. If for no other reason than that, he was considered to be extremely dangerous.

She didn't know who Sheriff Gibbs was referring to when he commented on the car in the driveway ahead of them. She assumed it was the man who had been in and out of the office so much recently. The gossip was that he was a former "Secret Agent" or something like that and was dating Sarah Stone. Beverly liked Sarah, whom she had met a few times after coming on board with the Sheriff's office. She hoped that nothing had happened to her.

Beverly had also known Rick Jemenez. Like most of the eligible young women in town, she had even dated him a few times. He was a nice guy and a gentleman. Not too many of them around these days. She was saddened by his death and was looking forward to bringing whoever killed him to justice. If the person they were after was Rick's killer then she hoped he was home and that they could bring the case to a quick closure.

Turning off the road they pulled onto the long driveway. Everything looked quiet at the house. Sheriff Gibbs sped down the driveway towards the house.   Deputy Richardson instinctively put her hand on her department issued hand gun. Was she ready for this, she asked herself. As they pulled closer, they could see that the front door of the house was open but there was no visible sign of life.

The Sheriff had the door open to the car before it came to a full stop and jumped out without a word to Beverly. She hurriedly opened her door to follow her boss, only to be restrained by her seat belt. Silently cursing herself, she unbuckled her belt and jumped out.

Chapter 22

As I parked the car next to the house I knew I was getting ahead of myself. I had no authority to try to gain access to the house. It would irritate the Sheriff that I didn't wait for him. I had intended to wait but, well, now I was here. I couldn't back out now, as I couldn't be sure if I was seen coming down the driveway or not.

Developing a cover for being there was not hard. I had used many ruses in the past to get a quick check of who was present at a house and to delay an occupant's departure. I carried a set of bogus credentials in my glove compartment of my car for such occasions. I had done so for years. The credentials identified me as being employed by an alleged company contracted by the government to conduct official inquiries. Depending on the location and timing, any scenario could be used. With any luck, the Sheriff would arrive while I was talking to the occupant of the house.

I walked up and knocked on the door. I couldn't see a buzzer for a door bell. There appeared to be a spot once used for a door bell that had since been covered and painted over. The entrance area looked unkempt as did the rest of the outside of house, and for that matter, the yard.

There was no answer so I knocked again, this time loud enough to ensure I could be heard. I stepped back and tried to get a sense if anyone was home. The windows of the house were covered by cheap pale curtains of some sort. They may have been sheets, I wasn't sure.

No one came to the door. I walked to the south side of the house to look for another entrance. There was none. I thought about walking to the back of the house, but decided to walk back to the front. As I did I thought I saw a curtain move in the window closest to the front door. It may have been my imagination, but it made the little hairs on my neck stand up. I quickly moved back to the front door. Nothing happened. I knocked again.

The door opened a crack. Whoever opened it had kept the chain secure so the door only opened a few inches. I saw no one but a muffled voice asked, "What do you want?"

"I am sorry to bother you, Mister." I paused for a moment to let him add a name if he wanted to. He did not. "I represent Alamo Research, a large company on contract with the federal government to do background investigations on individuals applying for work with the United States government."

"You got the wrong house. No one here wants to work for the government." The voice stated emphatically and the door started to close.

"Excuse me," I responded and took a chance by holding the door open with my hand, "I am not interested in anyone living here, I am checking up on an individual named Joe Black. He worked as a ranch hand on the ranch across the road over there."

"Never heard of him," the voice said again.

I rushed into my next series of questions. I didn't want to give him a chance to close the door. When I pointed across the street I looked down the road. Where was the Sheriff, I thought. "That is okay, Mister," I said. "If you never heard of him, then you never heard anything bad about him. That's half of what we are hired to find out. No bad news is almost as good as some good news. You know how that works out. Please bear with me, just a few last questions then." I glanced down, just by chance, and saw something that took my breath away. I tried not to show a reaction. Hiding behind the door, I didn't think he could see me anyway. Just inside the door, on the floor, was a small puddle of blood that was just starting to dry. "I just need your name for my report. Can you spell your last name sir?" I was hoping my voice didn't sound any different.

For a second there was no sound at all from the other side of the door. A name was finally given. It was not Bill White or any variation there of, but I would have been shocked if it had been, even if the voice was that of White. I wasn't even sure if White was here. My goal was to find Sarah. If White had an accomplice, so be it. One rat was as bad as another.

"And how long have you lived here?"

"None of your business, I really must go. I can't say anything about your Mr. Brown or Black. I didn't know him." Again the door started to shut.

"How about a Mr. Bill White?" I couldn't resist and I didn't want to lose him.

The door stopped moving. The chain lock was removed and the door started to open. I still saw no one but the end of a barrel of what I believed to be a handgun of some sort edged past the door for a second.

It was all I needed, I slammed the door open and dove at the gun. The door crashed into the man on the other side hitting his left shoulder and side, knocking him backward. He tried desperately to bring the pistol up and fire at me but I was on his right arm too fast. The gun went off but fired into the floor.

I pulled him down on top of me as we fell. I had both hands on his gun arm which meant he had one arm free. He quickly realized this and began hitting me hard first in the side and then on the back of my head. I worked hard on the hand with the gun while at the same time I tried to roll the guy off me. He finally released the gun when he realized he had no choice. I was about to break a couple of fingers. But I was having less success in getting him off me and the blows were taking their toll. He was hanging onto my back and swung his free arm around my neck and started to choke me. I struggled to get my legs under me in a crouch and stood up quickly. Simultaneously, I smashed the guy into the wall. The house seemed to rattle but he barely loosened his grip. I rammed my left elbow into his gut and his grip again slipped, but now he had both hands free. He slammed his right hand against the side of my head. The blow stunned me and I started to stumble forward. The effect was only for a second. I took advantage of my downward and forward momentum to drop down and try to flip him off of my back.

My training had been many years earlier but I had always been a good student. He went flying over me and crashed into a chair. He was up fast though. I had taken a brief look around in search of the gun, it was behind me. I turned and hustled back to it and was leaning over when he leapt back onto my back. This was definitely getting old and dangerous. The gun scooted away as I kicked it by accident.

His grip this time wasn't as good and I was quickly able to get him off me. I hit him hard in the face with my right fist and he fell backwards towards the front door. At that point I heard screaming coming from somewhere below me. It was a woman.

He saw my reaction and my hesitation. "You will never get to her in time." He smiled and bolted through the open front door. I chased after him. As I went through the door I saw Sheriff Gibbs just stepping out of his car in the driveway. The guy running away was heading the other direction and was just disappearing behind the side of the house.

I shouted at Gibbs. "Go after him, Sarah is in here and she is hurt."

Gibbs turned to a deputy getting out from the passenger side and told her to call in for back-up. He then took off running in the direction of my assailant. "I saw him," he said as he passed me - I guess to reassure me he knew who he was chasing.

I turned and went back into the house. "Sarah!" I shouted. There was no sound. I hoped I was not too late. Plus, I hoped that the scream I had heard had indeed come from Sarah.

Deputy Beverly Richardson used the car radio to call in the need for back-up and for an ambulance. The radio call just took a few seconds. She had seen Sheriff Gibbs run off after the suspect. As they had stopped the car next to the others in the driveway, they both saw a man run from the house. The man had seen them, too.

Although she had not observed a weapon on the suspect, she knew one golden rule in law enforcement was not to let your partner go into harm's way without backing him up. She might be able to help out in the house, but the real danger was outside and her Sheriff was chasing it alone. She took off running in the direction she saw Sheriff Gibbs go a moment before.

She was not a fast runner but she worked out routinely and was in good shape. She was determined not to stop running until she caught up with Sheriff Gibbs. Hopefully he would be unhurt. She didn't want to think of the other possibilities. Her adrenaline was definitely in overdrive today.

As she rounded the house she saw Sheriff Gibbs nearly a hundred yards ahead of her. She didn't see the suspect. He must be behind the rise Sheriff Gibbs was just disappearing behind. She tried to run faster. Even though the terrain seemed fairly flat, there were sufficient gullies and underbrush for a person to hide in or for that matter to get lost in.

She crossed over the top of the small rise and caught a glimpse of someone jumping down into a gully or ditch a hundred or so yards ahead. She resolutely headed towards that point.

For his part, Bill took off running like a hunted animal. He knew his life was at stake. He had the advantage of knowing this area. There were not many places to hide and he knew it would be even harder to get to somewhere that would facilitate ultimate escape. As he was running a possible strategy came to mind. To effectively accomplish his plan, however, he would have to successfully double back to his house and to the small shed in his backyard. He wished now he had thought of it before he left the immediate vicinity of his yard. In his shed he always kept a loaded pump action shot gun. With it he would have a definite chance to fight his way to his car. Getting to his car was critical to escaping. Getting rid of the witnesses, all of them, was also now important. Without them he knew no one would still be able to identify him. At least they would not readily recognize him. He figured other cops were coming but until they arrived he still had a chance.

Bill jumped into a small creek bed and starting running along it as it curled back towards his house. There was movement behind him. Someone was gaining on him. He had taken a quick glance backwards and had only seen one person. He shot around a sharp bend and stopped listening to the approaching foot steps. He reached down and picked up a softball size rock. Maybe he would not have to get all the way back to the house to get a gun. Crouching down low, he was determined to crush the skull of the first person to come around the corner.

When Sheriff Gibbs started running after the man he believed to be Bill White, he did so determined not to let his suspect escape. He ran like a man obsessed. Indeed he was. The person running ahead of him was responsible, at least in some part, for the murders in the town he had sworn to protect. Three people had been killed right under his nose and now maybe a fourth. He knew all the victims well. Sheriff Gibbs believed if White escaped now to kill again it would only be because he failed to capture him when he had him in his grasp. The fact that White had a good lead on him or knew the terrain better was irrelevant, Sheriff Gibbs was determined to stay on his trail like a bloodhound until he caught up with him.

Gibbs ran with his 9mm Berretta in his hand but he did not want to have to shoot the man he was chasing. He needed to be sure that he was in fact White and, if so, to discover who else was involved in the killings. Sarah was apparently in the house so the question to her whereabouts was answered.

Gibbs believed that White was unarmed but he had no illusions that he would not be dangerous. As far as Gibbs was concerned, White had proved himself to be a cold-blooded killer. He would find a weapon or come at the Sheriff without one with a desire to kill with his bare hands. Gibbs also started to think that White could even have a weapon hidden out here somewhere for just such a situation.

White kept disappearing and reappearing in front of him. Gibbs felt he was gaining on him. As he jumped down into a creek bed and started following White, the trail turned back to the north and Gibbs realized that White was possibly doubling back to the house. He was concerned that Deputy Richardson and the rest may be caught by surprise. He picked his speed up as much as he could and started fumbling for his radio. He did not want to lose sight of White and did not want to get himself distracted with talking on the radio so he decided against making the call at this point. If they broke out of the creek and headed back to the house he thought he would have time to give them a few seconds heads up. That's all it should take. He came to another bend in the creek bed and raced around it at full speed.

As Deputy Richardson ran up towards the creek bed she saw the top of Sheriff Gibbs' head as it moved perpendicular to her in the creek bed. She turned diagonally to make up some ground. Good, she thought the trail of the creek bed would allow her a better chance to catch them. A thought suddenly exploded in her mind. If White was also in the creek bed ahead of the Sheriff, which was likely, she could actually run parallel to the Sheriff and intercept them both where the creek bed turned back towards the house and the road.

Initially concerned that she would run into White first, she quickly realized that Sheriff Gibbs was running faster than she was. She would likely just run into him just after the bend in the creek bed. She looked frantically ahead for any sign of the suspect but could see none. He must not be as tall as the Sheriff she thought. Deputy Richardson, like Sheriff Gibbs, ran with the assumption that the suspect was unarmed. He would have likely fired at someone by now if he had been armed. Still, she knew he would be very dangerous.

Thinking this, she suddenly realized that she had been running without drawing her weapon and was rapidly approaching the creek bed where she could run right into the suspect. She looked down and quickly unholstered her hand gun. As she did so she did not see a large gopher hole that her right foot caught squarely. As a result she went flying onto the ground ahead of her, hitting a wet muddy patch of ground first with her face, then sliding through it with the rest of her body. She jumped back up, dirty but unhurt. She still had her weapon in her hand. At least she didn't drop that. She continued her pursuit of the others hoping that she had not lost too much ground. Embarrassed as she was, she knew she had no choice but to keep going.

As Sheriff Gibbs rounded the bend in the creek bed he

suddenly saw a figure leap at him.   It was White.   Gibbs instantly realized that White was trying to strike him with a large rock. Gibbs ducked, turned and did all he could to avoid the blow but White was on top of him too fast. The rock came crashing down on him.

Bill White frantically struck at the figure that bolted around the corner. The Sheriff came faster than he anticipated and reacted quicker to his assault than he thought possible. But he still had the element of surprise and was able to land a vicious blow hitting the sheriff's shoulder rather than his head. Sheriff Gibbs let escape a muffled scream of pain as the rock broke bone and tore at muscle.

The Sheriff fell to the ground and rolled. The pain was excruciating but he did not want to give White a stationary target to strike at again. White struck at him again just missing his head. Gibbs was relieved that White was going for the kill rather than just striking him anywhere. The rock would have done tremendous damage to any part of his body. It would not take too many blows to completely immobilize him.

The Sheriff's gun went flying with the first blow and he had no idea where it was. Gibbs tried whatever he could to stay away from the rock. He kicked White hard knocking him briefly away. Gibbs tried to stand up but White recovered too quickly from the kick and ran up to him striking Gibbs with what was fortunately just a glancing blow to the head. But it was enough, Gibbs went down. He again tried to kick White but his foot just glanced off White's thigh. White moved in, raising the rock above his head. Gibbs knew he would have to deflect the rock but White was coming in on the side of his bad shoulder.

The rock came flying down as White threw it instead of just striking the Sheriff with it. Gibbs tried to dodge the stone the best he could but it glanced off the side of his face as it hit the ground. The stone tore some skin and Gibbs thought it may have cracked his jaw but he was still conscious. Gibbs pushed himself backwards and away from White. He tried to stand up but stumbled awkwardly backwards. When he looked back up he saw that his luck had really run out as White had leaned over and picked up his Berretta.

"Hold on, you don't want to do that," Sheriff Gibbs futilely instructed White.

Bill White, however, was not listening. He raised the weapon and aimed it at the Sheriff.

Gibbs knew White was too close to miss. He looked quickly around but there was nowhere to go, nowhere to hide.

White smiled, he never really doubted that everything would fall back into his favor. Shoot the man in front of him, then get his shot gun and kill the remaining witnesses. He could be on the road to Mexico in five minutes. He aimed the Beretta at the man's chest. He realized he was about to shoot a law enforcement officer, but he didn't know specifically who it was. Even if he had, it would not have mattered. Kill or be killed he thought.

Chapter 23

Inside the house, I leaned over and picked up the gun off the floor. I tucked it into my belt. I learned long ago to never leave a weapon lying about.

"Sarah!" I shouted again.

"Help, down here!" It sounded like Sarah.

"I'm coming, everything is okay now," I shouted. I knew it really wasn't. Nothing would be totally safe until the individual fleeing from Gibbs, who I thought was White, and his elderly accomplice were captured.

I looked around for a way to get downstairs. Whoever owned this house was definitely not into housekeeping. The house smelled of something rotten and dust and debris were abundant. I finally found a door off the kitchen that went down to a basement. There was nothing there, though.

"Sarah!" I shouted again.

"In here!" came her response. "Hurry!"

The urgency in her shout hit me hard in the pit of my stomach. White had told me I was too late. If she was dying, I did not have a moment to spare. But I could not see how I could get to the sound. The basement was cluttered with boxes and shelves. Her voice had come from behind the wall to my right. I went over and started moving boxes. After looking around and behind the boxes, I realized that a shelving unit filled with paint cans and other heavy objects was actually a foot or two away from the wall. At first glance, with all the clutter, it would seem unlikely that a door would be hidden behind the shelf due to the effort it would take to move it.

Once up close to it though, I saw I could get behind the shelves and I saw the door. It opened inward allowing a person to easily slip behind the shelves and enter the room. The room was dark and not much light was allowed through from the room I had just come from.

The silhouettes in front of me looked ghoulish. The room stunk with a combination of odors I had only experienced a few times before. It was an odor I tried hard to forget.

"Jim, is that you?" Sarah asked. I could sense some trembling in her voice. I also realized she was one of the dark silhouettes hanging there in front of me.

"Yes," I said. "Where is the light switch?"

"By the door somewhere," she responded. "But you must call an ambulance first. There is another girl here hurt badly. I am not even sure if she is still alive."

"I think one is already coming," I answered. I found the switch. It had actually been on the wall outside the door.

I was momentarily stunned when I saw the inside of the room. The blood was everywhere. There was a crumbled body in the corner directly in front of the door. While Sarah looked pitiful hanging there from the ceiling bloody and bruised, the young girl hanging next to her looked like something out of one of the forensic books I had studied long ago of a person brutally tortured to death. Her back was badly bruised and cut. Blood was oozing slowly down her body from a number of wounds.

I rushed forward and instinctively worked on Sarah's bonds.

There was no way I would be able to free the chains without finding the key that was used on the small lock that held the chains together. I did see where the chains went to the side wall and down to a metal post that held the victim at a specific height. I was able to release that and let Sarah down. She moaned in pain as the pressure was released from her shoulders and wrists. A quick glance at her and I did not see any wound that looked major, but I knew a doctor would be needed to make sure of that. Who knew what internal injuries she might have?

She was able to stand on her own and told me to hurry with the other young woman hanging there so pitifully. Sarah helped ease the other woman down as I released her chain. She spoke to her softly calling her Tiffany. However, Tiffany was unconscious and slowly collapsed onto the filthy floor.

"Check the tool box for the key. I think he keeps everything he needs in it." Sarah instructed with urgency.

"Jesus," I muttered to myself. The inside of the toolbox was covered with new and dried blood.

"Where's White?" Sarah asked apprehensively.

"He took off running, trying to escape. The Sheriff's after him now. Don't worry he won't be coming back here. There is also a deputy out there who called for back-up." I couldn't blame her for still being frightened.

I found a key ring in the tool box with two small keys attached. They looked like the type that would go with the small locks holding the chains together.

"I think these are what we need." I took the keys over to Sarah first. "Who is the guy in the corner? And, I am assuming by the way he is lying there that he is dead. I guess I ought to check."

I didn't want to. The way he was lying all twisted up unnaturally gave him a sad but morbid look.

"You don't need to, he is dead. Tiffany said White killed him and since I have been here he has not moved a muscle. Most of this blood is his." Sarah motioned to the floor under the spot where she had been hung.

In short order Sarah was standing there rubbing her wrists and I was bent over trying to find the lock and keyhole in the chains that bound Tiffany. I felt great pity for this poor girl who I believed to be dying. It took me a few moments to find the lock and to release it.

"We need to get her off the floor and to some place clean." I commented. "This whole house is filthy." I muttered mostly to myself.

At that moment I heard the muffled sound of a gun being fired somewhere outside. The first shot was followed shortly after with a second. It actually sounded closer than I would have thought by now. I was instantly concerned with the thought that they were coming back towards the house.

Sarah heard it, too. "God, let's hope that was the Sheriff doing the shooting."

"Well, I have White's gun." I said tapping the barrel of it. "So unless he was able to get to another one, it should have been." I tried to sound confident, but I was worried. There were too many ways that White could get his hands on another weapon. His taking one from the Sheriff or the deputy was a possibility that I also couldn't readily shake from my imagination.

"So that was White?" I asked as I was picking up Tiffany's limp form from the floor. "It looks like most of her bleeding has slowed." Not necessarily a good sign though, I thought.

"Yes," Sarah responded to my question about White. "The guy is totally insane. You know the stories about the missing hitch-hikers and other transients." It wasn't a question and I knew immediately where she was leading.

"You mean White was responsible for those, too?"

"Yes," she said and then paused. "My guess is there are a number of bodies buried around here somewhere."

I had difficulty squeezing out the door and along the shelves while carrying Tiffany. White probably dragged his victims through the narrow passageway. Sarah walked hesitantly in front of me.

"We need to get you some clothes."

"I am not letting anything of White's touch my body," was her very adamant response.

"Once we get Tiffany upstairs you can have my wind breaker. I think the couch in the living room may be the best place to lay her down until the ambulance arrives. From the appearance of the rest of the house I would hate to think what his bed looks like. I have a blanket in the car we can use to cover her."

I looked down into the face of the young girl I was carrying. She looked peaceful and I wondered if somehow she knew her torment was over, one way or the other.

"You are going to be okay now Tiffany," I said softly.

Sarah heard me and turned around to give me a look of

support.   Looking back at her, I momentarily let my mind wander from the tragic situation we were in to think about what an interesting character this Sarah Stone truly was. Despite all she had been through, she was more concerned about Tiffany than herself and determinedly defiant when it came to her kidnapper.

We laid Tiffany down on the couch as she was starting to regain consciousness. That was a good sign I thought. She looked up at me and then over to Sarah. She seemed to smile and then slipped back into unconsciousness.

"Here, take this." I said offering her my light jacket. "I am not sure how much good it will do you."

"We need to try to clean her wounds the best we can and to stop her bleeding," was Sarah's response.

I looked around for a phone. "Where the hell is the ambulance and the other back-up?" I asked in frustration, knowing well that Sarah wouldn't know and that it was probably just minutes out. I saw the phone on the floor next to an old side table and under a lamp. As I moved to it, I heard the back door being opened.

Sarah heard it, too, and gasped out loud.

"Who is it?" She frantically whispered to me.

I drew White's gun from my belt and instinctively crouched. Someone was coming through the house quickly.

Chapter 24

Deputy Richardson ran as fast as she could to the creek bed. She thought she had heard something when she fell, but she could not be sure. She felt like an idiot falling like that but there was no time to dwell on her misstep.

She wiped a piece of wet dirt away from her left eye as it had started to blur her vision. She hoped it was just dirt. Running and blinking she came to the edge of the creek bed. She looked down the creek bed as it ran by the house and to the road and saw nothing. Quickly turning to look the other direction, she saw them. White was just hurling something down at Sheriff Gibbs but it looked like it missed. A large rock, she thought. She raised her issued 9mm Berretta and tried to aim it at White. He moved too fast and then reached down to pick up something. Another rock? No, she realized it was a hand gun.

She aimed at White just as he was beginning to aim at the Sheriff.

"Drop it!" Deputy Richardson shouted, "Now!"

White heard her. He turned his head but held the gun aimed in the direction of the injured Sheriff. At first he wasn't sure at what or at whom he was looking. The person, a female disheveled and covered with mud, was pointing a gun at him. She was wearing some form of a uniform, but both her uniform and her face were camouflaged. In a way she reminded him of a camouflaged soldier, maybe a Marine. White fought to regain control of his racing imagination, it didn't make sense.

White had a couple of choices. He could shoot the Sheriff and then try his luck with the woman with the gun. He could try to turn and shoot the woman, then turn back to the Sheriff. Two quick shots, either way. The third option, he could surrender. This last choice was entirely out of the question.

He stared hard at the female pointing the gun at him. She was nearly fifteen yards away. Even at that distance he could see the end of the hand gun shaking. He grinned at her. If it was only possible to wound her and then take her to his basement he thought. But there was no time. He would simply have to kill them both then get back to the house. There he would kill everyone else and leave immediately. He had to survive. For the time being he was the hunted animal. He had been in this role before and he knew what he had to do. He was back in control.

Deputy Richardson was frightened. She wanted to yell again at White, to order him one more time to drop his weapon, but she didn't think she could talk without letting him know how frightened she actually was. She would be lucky to be able to talk at all. She fully comprehended that White was weighing the odds. At some point, Deputy Beverly Richardson realized that this suspect was not going to surrender and that she was going to have to fire or let him shoot the Sheriff and possibly her. She steeled herself to this fact just as White spun to fire his weapon at her.

Chapter 25

I hadn't fired a weapon in a long time, even for practice, but I was confident in these close quarters I would not miss. I waved at Sarah to get her to duck behind something and crouched down ready for White to come running into the room.

Coming around the corner, however, was not White. It was Deputy Richardson, who stopped dead in her tracks when she saw me. She started to raise her weapon and in that instant I realized that she really did not know who I was. She had probably seen me a few times but I was not someone she knew. As she started to raise the 9mm in her hands all I could think of was that in her panic she would shoot me.

I quickly dropped the gun from my hands and raised both in a sign of surrender. I could see that she was in an extremely high state of anxiety. She also looked completely disheveled and covered with mud. I thought she must have already been through one hell of a fight.

Sarah shouted, "Beverly, it's all right! He's one of the good guys." In doing so I think she may have saved me from being shot.

Beverly lowered her weapon and the look of relief was obvious on her face. She looked at Sarah and then Tiffany on the couch.

"Oh, my God," was all Deputy Beverly Richardson could

say at first.

The sound of a siren, an ambulance I hoped, could be heard coming from the direction of town. It would be here momentarily.

Beverly walked up to Sarah and asked in a low voice, "Are you okay? You look pretty beat up."

"I'll be fine," Sarah responded. "I am very concerned about Tiffany, though. She has had a very rough time."

"What happened out there? Did you all get White?" I asked.

Deputy Richardson turned back to me and answered. "Yes, the Sheriff has him covered at the moment. White's not going anywhere. The Sheriff is hurt, but he will be okay."

Sarah was roaming around looking for something. She found what she was looking for, her clothes. They were in the trash in the kitchen. Apparently White disposed of the clothing of his victims in the trash, probably then burning them with his own trash in a barrel or pit somewhere. As she was putting on the few items of clothing that were not cut up to the point of being useless and Deputy Richardson was covering Tiffany with a blanket she found in a closet, I went out the back door to see if I could help the Sheriff.

As I got a few yards away from the house, I could see an ambulance, along with another Sheriff's patrol car speeding towards us just a half mile away. I walked out to the creek bed and saw the Sheriff and White. Gibbs had propped himself up in a semi-sitting position against a steep edge of the embankment. White was a few yards away lying prone. He wasn't moving so I wondered if he was conscious.

Gibbs didn't notice me until I got close. When he did, he

looked at me inquisitively. "How is Sarah?"

"Hurt, but in good spirits right now. She will be all right. There were two other people in the basement. One, a young man is dead. The other is a young woman, probably just a teenager. I believe she may also be dying, if not dead, already. You look a mess, are you all right?"

"I'll be fine," Gibbs answered.

"The scarring will just make you look more manly anyway." I said in a jesting manner. He grinned back at me.

"Those inside, victims of his, I presume?" He asked, tilting his head towards the prone figure of White.

I nodded. "From what Sarah mentioned, I think this guy may also be the suspect the FBI is looking for with regards to some of the missing hitch hikers. Is he alive?" After asking the question, I figured it was a dumb one since Sheriff Gibbs was sitting there watching him with a gun in his hands, but I didn't know if anyone had actually checked him for life signs.

"He was a minute ago. If you want to check him out, go ahead. He may have a weapon on him but I doubt it. He attacked me with a rock. Likely would have killed me if it wasn't for Beverly. You should have seen her. God, I wished I could have caught it on video. Deputy Richardson certainly impressed me, standing there facing down an armed maniac. He had my gun, I'm embarrassed to say. She stood over there, all mud faced and breathing hard. My guess is that this sucker here thought she would be an easy kill. His only decision was who to shoot first, me or her. Thankfully he decided to go for her first. He could have killed me easy. He wasn't but a few yards away. But that would have given her a free shot. He played the odds correctly but lost. She fired and hit him plug in the chest. He staggered for a second, fired one shot into the ground and collapsed."

I walked over to where he was lying. He was unconscious and breathing poorly. I gave Gibbs my diagnosis. "I think the bullet took out a lung." There was blood smeared along the ground for a few feet.

Gibbs could see where I was looking. "He crawled there from a few feet to your left a minute ago and then passed out. Is he losing a lot of blood?"

"Hard to say until someone rolls him over," I patted him down and could not find a weapon. There was also no wallet or other identification.

"But he is alive and will probably make it. If his heart or a major artery were hit, he would probably be dead by now."

I looked up and saw a male deputy and medical technician, or possibly a doctor, coming towards us from the house.

"Is someone taking care of the women inside?" I shouted.

"Yes. Who all needs help out here," responded the deputy.

"Just me and the killer, Wally," shouted the Sheriff. "I would recognize that voice anywhere," he added softly to me.

"Where are you Sheriff? I can't see you," asked the deputy whom Gibbs referred to as Wally.

"Over here," I answered. They could see me, but as neither Gibbs nor White were standing they were still out of sight.

The deputy and the medic jumped down into the creek bed.

"How are the two women at the house?" I asked.

"They are both alive. The younger gal is seriously hurt though. She may not make it," answered the medic. I had decided he wasn't a doctor. "They are going to take them back to Denton right now. I think they will have to call in a helicopter from Albuquerque or Santa Fe to get that young gal to a hospital that can do a lot more for her than our small clinic. Sarah should be okay with our hospital here in Denton. She didn't think that she had any critical injuries."

The medic looked first at Sheriff Gibbs. He wasn't hurt as badly as White but no one seemed to care. The medic opened his kit and pulled out a sling. Despite some pain they were able to get the Sheriff into a tight fitting sling that held his arm and shoulder in place.

"I may not be a doctor," the medic said to the Sheriff, "but I believe something is busted up there." He motioned to the Sheriff's shoulder. "I also think you need some stitches to close that nasty gash in your face. You already have a nasty bruise on your cheek but I don't think your jaw is broken."

The Sheriff smiled, "Buck, I still can't figure out why you didn't become a brain surgeon." He winked at me. Hurt as badly as he was, the Sheriff definitely seemed to be in good spirits. I also noted that there was a genuine affection between the medic and the Sheriff, much like there was between most everyone I had seen with the Sheriff. I couldn't help but be impressed.

"How about you, Jim? Any injuries that Buck, here, could operate on?" Gibbs asked me. It was easy to see that no one was in a hurry to help out White. I guess I couldn't blame them, but he did need some attention.

"No, I'm fine." I answered. "But you better do something to keep him alive. I would think it might be good if we could get some type of confession out of him.   Sarah thinks he is responsible for a number of the missing hitch hikers that the FBI has been looking for. In fact, her theory is that the bodies may be buried out here somewhere."

Sheriff Gibbs looked at Buck. "You heard him, get to work and save that bum's lousy life, Doc."

Buck ambled over to the body on the ground. The Deputy had already been over White, patting him down again for weapons or ID.   He had also handcuffed the limp body. Probably the prudent thing to do, but he wasn't going anywhere.

"Wally, stay here with Buck and keep an eye on this guy." He motioned at White. "He may have a lot more to answer for than just the killings in Denton. Plus wasn't there supposed to be an older fellow here, too?" He directed this question to me.

"I am starting to have my doubts about that." I wasn't sure but something bothersome was bugging me with the thought that there may not be a second person. Maybe it was the layout in the house, the single car in the driveway, the implication by Sarah that White was responsible for many additional killings. Some pieces were still out of place, but it was all starting to unravel for White. I had no doubt the Sheriff, with the FBI's help would be getting to the bottom of it.

Sheriff Gibbs was standing up with Wally's assistance. Once he was up he stood still for a moment. "Okay, I am good to go. Let's get back to my car. I have some people I want to contact." He started walking toward the house. I walked with him. I offered him my arm for support but he claimed he didn't need it.

The ambulance was already racing back to Denton. We could see it disappearing down the road. I hoped Sarah was in the ambulance with Tiffany. Whether she acknowledged it or not, she had some injuries that needed a doctor's attention.

As we approached the house, a second deputy came out. This one I recognized as the one who had surprised me in front of Luke's house when I first arrived in Denton. "Sheriff, I let the ambulance go back with the two women. They needed quick attention, especially the younger one. Beverley went back with them. I thought that would be more appropriate, too, than one of us going along."

"Good thinking, Rick," answered Gibbs. "I need you to carefully double check every room in the house. Make sure there is no one else in there. Don't be looking for evidence of a crime at this point. We first need to make sure there isn't a second suspect in there. There was some talk of an older person living here. Once you are sure no one else is in the house, you can secure it for forensics. Understand?"

"There is another body in the basement. A young man I believe. And," I added, "a lot of blood. Other than that, I think the house is empty."

"Jesus," uttered Rick. He turned and went back into the house.

"Who were the other victims?" the Sheriff inquired.

"I only have a part of the story, but apparently a couple of kids who were bumming rides, illegally, on trains. As I mentioned, Sarah believes that the guy lying out there in the creek bed is responsible for a number of the missing people that are at the heart of a major nationwide FBI investigation."

"Amazing," was all Gibbs said. When we got to his car, he pulled out the microphone to his mobile radio and called back to his office in town. He was acknowledged right away.

Sheriff Gibbs further impressed me that morning. Despite his injuries, he set in motion a concept of operations to handle the situation that was sound and comprehensive. He ensured that the FBI was already notified and on their way. He did not waiver indecisively worrying that the FBI might second guess him like I've seen so many times before with other law enforcement agencies and officials. He passed out instructions for a good ten minutes, often having to repeat himself to clarify questions. When he finished, he sat down exhausted on the passenger seat of the car.

Just then two more deputy vehicles pulled up next to us along with another ambulance. It seemed at first that they were all late getting here until I realized that I had only arrived twenty minutes or so earlier. A lot had happened in that time.

The deputies were wandering around the outside of the house, reluctant to go inside without the Sheriff's instruction. The new medics came over to look at the Sheriff. He wasn't in the mood for further help.

"I'm okay. Go out back and get our prisoner. He's hurt real bad but we need to keep him alive. If, for no other reason, to help us find out how many people he may have killed and where he may have buried them." Gibbs instructions were to all of them. "He is in the creek bed maybe fifty yards behind the right side of the house. Wally is with him. Jim and I will stay here and keep anyone drifting by out of the house."

The whole troop hurried around the house per the Sheriff's instructions.

"They're a bunch of good folk," he commented, as much to himself as to me.

Chapter 26

The rest of the day seemed to go on for ever. The scene at the house changed from that of a lonely small structure in the middle of nowhere to the center of great focus and attention. Dozens of law enforcement personnel from all over the country and from many different jurisdictions showed up to help local authorities and to protect their own equities in cases in which they had their own interest.

Overall it was impressive to watch. The cooperation between the agencies was very good. Political fights might occur later, but at this juncture everyone worked well together.

As the Sheriff refused to leave, a doctor from town actually drove out to the scene to take a look at him. His diagnosis was that it wasn't so much the shoulder that was damaged as it was the collar bone. As such, as long as the Sheriff took it easy the treatment could wait until that night. Not as though the doctor had much choice anyway, but to wait. The gash on Sheriff Gibbs' face was cleaned and temporarily bandaged.

I was happy that the Sheriff never criticized me for going to the house alone ahead of every one else. He would have been right to have done so, but rather than chastise me at all, he routinely introduced me as the hero of the day. I didn't need or even want the praise but it did feel good.

For all the good that the Sheriff could do for me, I was able to embarrass myself on my own fairly effectively. In the middle of the afternoon, hours after the search began, two of the Sheriff's deputies came out to him and informed him that they had looked everywhere but could not find a hand gun that might match the one used on Rick, Luke and his grandmother. As soon as they said this to Gibbs, I realized why they had not been able to find it. I had it on my person tucked into my belt. I had picked it up in the house and had never released it.

Embarrassed, I handed over the gun to them. They immediately wanted to know why I had it and how I had gotten it.

"Slow down, guys." Gibbs quickly jumped in. "It is a long story and you weren't here for the beginning. We'll get Mr. West's statement later. Right now tag the weapon and then get it back to forensics on the next run."

Content, the deputies left.

"Sorry about that."

"No biggie," he said to me with a smile.

Chapter 27

It was getting dark when I finally arrived at the Denton Municipal Medical Clinic. As the name implied, it was not a major hospital. However, to its credit, I thought it looked fairly elaborate. I was to learn later that the reason it was not referred to as a hospital is that it lacked a number of care and diagnostic features of a larger hospital. It was sufficient to care for Sarah though. The doctors cleaned and dressed her wounds. They had given her something for the pain while they were working on her and it had knocked her out.

She had just awakened when I arrived but she had to stay at the clinic until the doctor gave her approval to leave. She seemed fine to me. In fact she looked beautiful. We chatted about her injuries and the day's excitement. The first thing she wanted to know, though, was how Tiffany was doing.

I knew no more than she did, that Tiffany had been flown to Albuquerque by helicopter.

Sarah also needed to be reassured that White had been captured and was no longer a danger to anyone. She had been there when Deputy Richardson had come running into the house and told us of her shooting White. She just needed his capture to have some finality, which I was certainly able to provide to her. In fact, he too had been taken by helicopter, along with an FBI agent and a deputy sheriff as escorts, to the same hospital in Albuquerque they had previously taken Tiffany.

The doctor, a young female around Sarah's age came into the room. She gave me an inquisitive glance.

"Who is the handsome stranger?" She asked Sarah with a smile.

Sarah introduced me to Judy Berg. The two had been acquaintances in school while growing up in Denton. A year apart in grade and living on opposite ends of town had interfered with their becoming closer at that time. Later, after they both started their professional careers in Denton, they had become good friends.

Judy asked me to leave so she could take one last look at Sarah's wounds before she released her.

"It's okay, he can stay." Sarah stated.

Again that inquisitive look from Doctor Berg.

"I'll just step outside," I said.

I did not have to wait long. Maybe five minutes after I got relaxed in a soft chair in the lobby just down the hall, both Sarah and Doctor Berg walked up.

"That was quick," I commented.

"Good news," Sarah stated with a smile. "Judy said they think Tiffany will pull through."

Sarah was dressed in a new black and gold jogging outfit. She looked marvelous.

"Nice outfit."

"My boss and some friends from the office came by earlier. They asked what I needed and something to wear was the only thing I could think of. Everyone has been so sweet to me. But don't you think it's great that Tiffany may pull through? That makes me so happy!"

"Yes, I am, too." I couldn't help but think that Tiffany was going to have a bit of psychological scarring to overcome, which might be just as difficult.

"You need to fill me in with what is happening out there at the house. Have they found any more bodies?" I was surprised by her inquisitiveness as I had imagined that she would want to put the whole incident as far behind her as possible.

She must have noticed something in my reaction because she quickly added, "It's the reporter in me. This is my story and I plan on writing something that will rock the whole state."

"The whole nation more likely," I said. "The investigation is focusing on the house at the moment. They have sealed off the property and I believe the investigative team will be bringing in some special equipment and some dogs to help out in the search for more bodies. I really don't have all the facts. I was present for a lot of the conversations that the Sheriff had with the FBI but I was a passive audience. I didn't take any notes."

"That's ok." She said with a big smile. She grabbed my hand, "I guess saving my life is a good enough thing for one day. But tomorrow you need to take better notes."

I had the feeling that she was only half kidding.

As we walked out of the hospital, I asked her where I could take her. I think being outside in the evening dusk and having to think about her options brought the long day's events back to her. She grabbed my arm a little tighter and said, "I don't know, but don't leave me alone tonight."

"Well I haven't eaten anything all day, other than a couple donuts brought out to the scene by one of the deputies. How about if we just go to the pancake house? I could sure use some eggs and coffee." I thought the atmosphere would be about as peaceful as one could find and, actually, the thought of some eggs and coffee did sound good.

"Let's do it," she answered.

I drove her over to the restaurant. When we walked in, everyone just stopped doing what they had been doing and stared at us. Just as suddenly though all the wait staff and even some of the customers got up and came over to us to see how we were. At least that was my initial thought. I quickly realized the entourage was interested in Sarah, not me. But that was just fine. It was how it was supposed to be. She was part of their family.

We were soon escorted to a table and everything got back to normal.

"You have a lot of friends," I complimented her.

"That's because I have lived here my whole life. The town isn't that big, you know." She tried to downplay her sudden celebrity status.

Just then, Dave and Saul came into the restaurant and sat down at a table.

"If you want to thank the two that really were the key to our finding you, you should go thank those two over there." I mentioned to her pointing at Dave and Saul. "They were the ones who mentioned to me that a person who could possibly be Bill White was seen at the house where I went to look for you. Without their lead we probably never would have gone there in time."

"I will, but that reminds me, whose house was that? It wasn't listed under his name, was it? I mean, didn't the Sheriff run a series of checks to see if White was living in the area. I assume that would have included electric utilities, real estate, etc."

"My guess is that we will discover that White was living there under an assumed name and probably traveling around under a disguise. They found some wigs and other stuff an actor might have to disguise appearance. They also found a lot of correspondence addressed to the house to someone other than White. There is no sign that a second person ever lived there. My guess no one ever did. He probably assumed the identity of one of his victims. Not that hard to do if you pick the right victim."

"Amazing! What a sick man," Sarah said in disgust.

She got up and walked over to the table where Saul and David were seated. They rose and Dave started to shake her hand but Sarah gave them both a hug instead. She pointed over to me. They both recognized me and waved. She gave me a sign to indicate she would be just a minute.

She returned a few minutes later. "I get the check tonight. Not just to thank you, I'm picking up theirs too."

"That was nice of you," I said.

"Guess I owe them. Plus, I hate to say this, but all I could think of since this morning was what a story this would make. I was terrified and thought I might die, but I couldn't shake the fact that this was also a once in a lifetime story and I was in the middle of it. Am I sick?" She asked me.

"No. Being a reporter is what you are. Representatives of the major television networks along with the major wire services were all showing up out of nowhere today at White's house.   We had trouble keeping them off the grounds.   I imagine once they start digging there will even be some press helicopters overhead taking photos.   I don't blame you at all. Just keep it all in perspective.   What is most important is that you and Tiffany are alive and that an insane serial killer is behind bars.   Once you fully understand the priorities, you'll see that the story is still very important but secondary to the welfare and safety of the victims."   I stopped myself because I knew if I didn't, I would end up preaching even more to her.

"Thanks."   I couldn't tell if I had hit a nerve.   She took a sip of water and stared at a far wall in thought.   Her eyes began to tear up a little.

"You know, I was terrified.   I was scared to death and I do understand what you are saying.   I don't disagree with you but I do want to pursue this story.   I think it is a way to chase the gremlins out of my mind.   I also want to tell Tiffany's story.   She is a brave kid.   She went through hell, probably more than I could ever handle.   It may help her too.   I don't think that is wrong."

"No, it isn't."   She had every right to do the story.

The waitress showed up with our order and we ate and talked about other things.   We sat and talked for a little over an hour.   It was a pleasant hour.   When we left, two of the waitresses gave her a hug and one of them even gave me one.

I drove her to her house.   When we got there she asked if I would come in with her.   It was easy to see that her bravado from dinner was only skin deep.   There were indeed some gremlins that needed chasing out.

Inside she gave me a tour of the house. My impression was that I was helping her ensure everything was safe. It was. She offered me a beer and we sat in her living room and talked. At first she sat on a large stuffed chair. I sat on the couch. Finally she came over to the couch and snuggled against me. She said she didn't want to be alone.

I stayed the night and did my best not to fall asleep too early this time.

Chapter 28

They found seventeen bodies buried in the field around Bill White's house. Even with the DNA checks that could be done, the FBI was only able to identify fifteen. The other two were presumed to be drifters that were never reported missing.

Tracking back the alias that White had used in Denton the authorities were able to take his past life to Washington D. C. Assuming that he may have taken on the identity of one of his earlier victims, the FBI hit the jackpot when they matched up White with Manuel "Manny" Johnson, one of his boat mates back in North Carolina. Tracing tax records on Manny Johnson the FBI discovered one with the same social security number who lived in Washington for an approximate period of time that matched the period after White disappeared off the coast in North Carolina and when he showed up in New Mexico. His employer in Washington was shown a photograph and confirmed that the Manny who worked for him was in fact White.

Further investigation in Washington began to link White with many of the unsolved murders in the capitol city. The linkage was weak, but not that weak. There was a statistical increase in unsolved murders during the period of time White was believed to have lived in the city. Many of the bodies were nude when they found them. Some of the later victims had shown signs of being drugged, now known to be a modus operandi used by White. Finally, there was the connection to the body found in the landfill and the one on the trash barge.

The North Carolina authorities reopened their case on White, now more sure than ever that he was responsible for the murders of three of their citizens, too.

Sheriff Gibbs became an instant celebrity throughout New Mexico. A number of the big city newspapers did articles on the local New Mexican Sheriff, playing up his personal role in solving a nation-wide murder mystery that had foiled a national task force for years. Even some out-of-state papers did stories on him, picking up the lead from Santa Fe. As I expected, Gibbs handled the instant fame very well. I doubt if any of it went to his head. As far as he was concerned, he just did what he was supposed to do and he certainly knew and said he didn't solve the case by himself.

One newspaper article in particular was a favorite among those in Denton and probably elsewhere in New Mexico. A Boston paper kept referring to the close cooperation between the FBI and the "Mexican" police, referring to the local Denton authorities. The Boston paper even expanded on this point to show that cooperation with the Mexican authorities in many border areas had historically been contentious. In response to this obvious geographic error, an elementary school student council in Denton sent a map of the United States to the newspaper's Boston editors with Denton, New Mexico, U.S.A., circled some two hundred miles north of the Mexican border.

Despite the recommendations of both the hospital and her editor to take some time off, Sarah dove straight into the story herself. She knew she had the inside track to an in-depth look at Bill White and she knew there would be a lot of major wire services and networks interested in such an expose. She spent a lot of time with Tiffany, who was recovering better than expected, picking her mind for statements that White made and other impressions that Tiffany developed regarding White. Sarah located a number of old friends that White had grown up with in Denton and verified his obsession with Annie Shell. She worked out a deal with her local paper and a couple of national wire services to put out short summary updates as she progressed. Before long a major television network learned of her wealth of info and started pressing her for an interview for a prime time news show. Sarah held off but strung them along. She knew it would take some time to put everything together, and she wanted to get it right.

Unfortunately White was not going to talk to anyone. Unconscious when they took him to the hospital, he subsequently died from internal hemorrhaging on the operating table. There were the typical criticisms by some of the lunatic fringe that claimed that the authorities had killed him on purpose. The official medical report, however, stated that the bullet had nicked a major artery close to the heart. The medical team did not realize the damage that had been done to the artery. When they started operating to repair his lung and chest cavity, the artery ruptured. There was nothing that could be done for him.

As far as my involvement with the remainder of the case, there was none. I left Denton the day after Sarah was released from the hospital. I stayed in touch with both Sheriff Gibbs and Sarah, even traveled back to Denton on a handful of occasions.

Sarah still was interested in seeing me and I found myself more and more interested in seeing her. But whereas I had plenty of free time on my hands, she was in the middle of what would likely be the busiest and most important project she may ever have as a reporter. The competition I faced was tougher than any other guy could have given me for her attention. She was even getting job offers from a number of big city newspapers. I invited her to spend a few days vacation with me in San Antonio, Texas. I told her she needed some time off and she said she would love to go with me, just not now.

I stay in touch; the story can't last forever.

Epilogue

I appreciate your patience as I told my story bouncing back and forth between first person and third person point of view. I only took that approach as it has been so long since the events occurred. Over that time frame, I have had several in-depth discussions with Sarah, Tiffany and Sheriff Gibbs regarding their memories of what transpired during those few terrible days. Sarah did extensive research on Bill White and I had access to those notes. The FBI also did a psychological profile on him. At the end, by the time I decided to write the story, I felt I couldn't omit everyone else's point of view.

Finally, to avoid answering numerous e-mails, my relationship with Sarah lasted about two years. It ended when she accepted a job with the Washington Post. We still stay in touch but she has moved on and I wish her the best. --- Jim West

Author Bob Doerr

Bob Doerr grew up in a military family, attended the Air Force Academy, and then had a career of his own in the Air Force. It was a life style that had him moving every three or four years, but also one that exposed him to the people and cultures of numerous countries in Asia, Europe and to most of these United States. In the Air Force, Bob specialized in criminal investigations and counterintelligence gaining significant insight to the worlds of crime, espionage and terrorism. In addition to his degree from the Academy he also has a Masters in International Relations from Creighton University. Bob now lives in Garden Ridge, Texas, with his wife of 36 years and their pet dog.

**To find out about new titles,
release dates, book signings,
speaking engagements and
other appearances visit**

www.bobdoerr.com

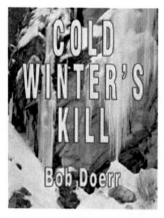

- Title: *Cold Winter's Kill*
- Author: Bob Doerr
- Price: $27.95
- Publisher: TotalRecall Publications, Inc.
- Format: HARDCOVER, 6.14" x 9.21"
- Number of pages: 288
- 13-digit ISBN: 978-1-59095-762-8
- Publication: Dec 8, 2009

COLD WINTER'S KILL is a fast paced thriller that takes place in the scenic mountains of Lincoln County, New Mexico and throws Jim West into a race against time to stop a psychopath who abducts and kills a young blonde every Christmas...

It was one of those phone calls former Air Force Special Agent Jim West never wanted to receive--an old friend calling to ask if he could drive down to Ruidoso, New Mexico to help locate his daughter who has disappeared while on a ski trip with friends. Jim found himself heading to Ruidoso even though he believed, much like the local authorities, that if she had gone missing in the mountains in December, her survival chances were slim. He didn't want to be there when they found her, but still he drove on.

Once in Ruidoso, Jim discovers a sinister coincidence that changes everything. It appears that someone is abducting and killing one young blond every year around Christmas. The race is on--can Jim locate his friend's daughter in time? But why is this happening and who's doing it?

Jim can't wait for the local authorities to raise the priority of their search, or for the pending blizzard to pass. In his haste he puts himself in the killer's sights. Will he, too, suffer from a cold winter's kill?

Advance Praise

"GREAT SUSPENSE! In *Cold Winter's Kill* Bob Doerr grabs your attention from the beginning and holds it until the last sentence. Hard to put down!"

> --Shelba Nicholson
> former Women's Editor, *Texarkana Gazette*

Author Bob Doerr Uses his special knowledge to provide authentic details in his novels about how law enforcement agencies do their work.

A Jim West™ Mystery/Thriller

LaVergne, TN USA
10 December 2009
166513LV00004B/4/P